Crushed

Barbara Ellen Brink

Barbara Ellen Brink

Visit Barbara Ellen Brink at www.barbaraellenbrink.com

Cover photo of vines © Katharine A Brink

Cover design by Katharine A. Brink

Author photo by Barbara E Brink

Edited by Nancy Hudson

ISBN-10:1461007283
ISBN-13:978-1461007289

DEDICATION

For my daughter Katharine, whose light shines
bright and makes my world a better place.

Another novel by this author
Entangled

CRUSHED

CHAPTER ONE

His voice, familiar as silk on skin, sent shockwaves through Margaret. The thick Italian accent she once swooned over was now polished to an aristocratic smoothness. She dropped the spatula she was flipping pancakes with, and turned to stare at the tiny television on the counter behind her.

"Of course Minor Hurricane is a long shot, but I have brought him to America to run and he shall certainly do so." Agosto Salvatore smoothed his tie and smiled at the camera with an impressive set of bleached teeth. He would make a perfect model for Esquire. He continued, "And I have no doubt he will rise to the occasion and surprise his competition."

The reporter appeared completely dazzled as though Europeans in Armani suits were worth much more than a dime a dozen. She asked, "Aside from the business of racing, do you have plans for a holiday during your stay in California?" Her expression said what her words did not, that she'd be more than happy to fit in with them.

He shrugged; one side of his mouth lifted. "Perhaps, but first I plan to visit my son."

Margaret gasped and stared numbly as the picture flashed to the racehorse in question, Minor Hurricane, being exercised by a groom.

"Thank you, Mr. Salvatore," the reporter's voice-over concluded. "And good luck to Minor Hurricane on Saturday. This is Jane Goodall with channel five news at the Golden Gate racetrack."

"Your pancakes are burning," Handel said as he strolled into the kitchen and set his briefcase on the floor by the door.

Margaret continued staring at the television screen.

"I didn't know toothpaste commercials could be so mesmerizing."

"You promised me I would never have to see him again." Her voice was soft, an undercurrent of hysteria running through it. "That Davy would never have to know him." She looked up and held her brother's gaze. Her lips trembled as she tried to gain control of her emotions. "Now what?"

***

"Now what?" Agosto folded his arms over the top of the fence and watched Minor Hurricane prance in a tight circle, defying the rider's instructions. The Jockey used his crop to get the horse's attention and Minor reared up in anger. Agosto frowned, and cursed under his breath. "What are you doing, Giuseppe? If you can't control him now, how in hell are you going to ride him to victory in the race on Saturday?" He felt a tap on his shoulder and turned from the fence.

One of the young men who worked in the stables stood there in filthy boots, a leather grooming-apron covered jeans and a t-shirt. "A guy wants to talk to you,

Mr. Salvatore. He's waiting over there." The teenager pointed past the buildings to the parking lot in the distance where a man stood with arms crossed, leaning against a red Porsche.

"Another reporter?" Agosto frowned in annoyance. He turned back to the fence in time to see his prize horse throw Giuseppe from the saddle. The jockey grabbed the reins before the stallion could run off. Agosto snorted his derision as the jockey was nearly knocked to the ground again. He glanced back. The boy was still waiting. "Tell him I don't want to give anymore interviews. Ms. Goodall was exclusive," he said, and smiled remembering just how exclusive.

The boy shook his head and held out a business card. "He's not a reporter. He's a lawyer. He said to give you this."

Agosto took the card, read the words, and glanced quickly toward the parking lot. "Tell him I'll be there in a moment."

The boy ran off and Agosto released a breath. He reached inside his suit coat for the silver cigarette case he normally kept there, but realized he'd left it in the hotel room earlier. "Damn." He patted his other pockets. None.

"Take Minor back to the stable and have him rubbed down," he ordered the jockey who had finally gotten the horse under control. He watched the pair canter down the track before he straightened his tie, slowly turned, and strolled toward his visitor.

The tall, blonde man took a step forward as Agosto approached, his gaze bold and direct even in the bright afternoon sun. Agosto saw a bit of Margaret in her brother's features, though broader in stroke. The familiar curve of the brow, wide mouth, and slanting eyes appeared rather ominous on Handel Parker, like an angry wolverine ready to pounce.

"Ciao, Handel! I'm surprised to see you here at the track. I didn't think you went in for racing or games of chance." Agosto held out his hand but Handel ignored it, the firm set of his lips and iciness of his gaze fair warning that this was far from a friendly visit to an old acquaintance.

"Why are you here, Salvatore?" Handel's question, blunt and to the point, put an end to formalities.

"I've come to see my son." He smoothed his hair with one hand, a nervous gesture that he stopped abruptly as he realized what he was doing. He hated feeling small and insecure, and Handel had always made him feel so. Margaret's brother, responsible, athletic, intelligent, and damn tall, was a thorn in his flesh. He would have to be taken out of the way before Margaret would listen to reason. "A boy needs his father to teach him to be a man." He waved an arm toward the track. "I can show him another world. He should know where he came from, what he's missing. My son should not have to live as though he has nothing when I can give him everything."

Handel leaned on one hip, his arms casually crossed over his chest. He let out a short, mirthless laugh and shook his head. "How do you expect to teach something you've never learned yourself?"

Agosto felt the sting of the words but held his tongue. There would be time enough for getting even. He sighed expressively and spread his hands in supplication. "I had hoped we could come to some sort of agreement for the boy's sake, but if you intend to fight me on this…" He let the unspoken challenge hang between them.

4

Handel straightened to his full height, pulled a pair of sunglasses out of his front pocket, slowly slipped them on. Precise movements of extreme control. "There's nothing to fight about. You have absolutely no connection to *the boy*. His birth certificate does not bear your name. You are nothing to him, and nothing to Margaret. You severed any ties you might have had when you ran off to Italy ten years ago, abandoning my sixteen-year-old sister as though she were nothing more than a rich boy's broken toy. If it weren't for my friendship with your cousin, you wouldn't be standing here today." Handel turned and opened the door of his car, revealing black leather interior and a rich wood console. He slid into the seat and twisted the key in the ignition. The engine roared to life. "Do yourself a favor and stay away from the Parker family." He slammed the door and hit the gas. The car's tires spun around on the concrete. A cloud of smoke lifted at his departure, and floated on the breeze toward the stables.

Agosto stared after the car for long seconds, his teeth clenched, his hands balled into fists at his sides. No one talked to him like that and got away with it. He glanced toward the paddock and saw the young groomer watching. He turned and strode across the parking lot toward his car, angry heat rising from his collar. Stay away from his own son? Handel Parker's ultimatum was a lot of hot air.

Agosto needed the boy. It was the only thing that would satisfy his father, who seemed to be in an all-out campaign to pressure him into producing an heir. His father had been pushing him toward marriage and a son as though the pope himself had ordained it. But his riding accident three years ago had caused more damage than anyone else knew. He would gladly appease the old man if that's what it took to have him relinquish control of the company, but an operation to reverse the damage proved fruitless; the doctors said there was nothing they could do. The son he conceived with Margaret Fredrickson was the only heir he would ever have. Nothing and no one could keep him from his own flesh and blood. The boy was his. Papers or no papers.

Perhaps he needed to go at this a little differently though. He let himself into the back of the limousine. Margaret was the key. She'd been head over heels for him ten years ago. She would be again.

The driver, dozing at the wheel, abruptly woke at the slamming of the door. He straightened and waited for instructions.

"Take me to the hotel," Agosto demanded and reached for a cigarette. He lit it and leaned back against the plush upholstery, inhaling deeply. After his nerves calmed, his thoughts were clear. Yes. Seducing Margaret again would not be hard. She was a lovely girl, most likely a beautiful woman. He stared out the window, but instead of scenery, sweet memories filled his vision…

Long blonde hair fell over his chest as they made love. The twin bed in her room creaked with their combined weight. Margaret smiled, leaned down, her breasts grazing his skin as she whispered the Italian words he taught her, words she is afraid to say too loud for fear someone will hear, words of lust and need. Later, she was pale and fragile beneath his hands when he moved above her, touching, caressing, teaching…

Agosto crushed his cigarette in the ashtray remembering Handel's sudden return from the winery that day. The interruption had been most unfortunate. He'd wanted Margaret to crave his touch like an addict, to scream for more until he was through with her. Perhaps this time he would have the chance to make her beg.

CHAPTER TWO

Adam strolled through the airport, his guitar strapped to his back, following straggling fellow passengers headed for baggage claim. People stood three deep around the carousel eagerly anticipating their first bag sighting. He slid the book he'd been reading on the plane out of his jacket pocket, and patiently waited on the outskirts of the mob.

"Here for vacation or coming home?" a woman asked beside him.

He looked up from the page he was on. In a short denim skirt, skintight tank top, and three-inch heels, the woman looked like man-candy on a stick. "An extended stay," he said, trying not to stare at the cleavage pouring from her neckline.

She reached across him, brushed his arm, and tipped the book up to read the title. "Ahh, you've come to tour wineries." Her lips curved into a teasing smile. "Don't stay too long. You won't be able to walk straight back onto the plane."

He closed the book with his finger in the page. "Thanks for the advice, but I'm not touring. I'm going to work at my sister's winery in the Napa Valley."

"Really? What's the name?" she asked, perfectly plucked brows raised with interest.

"Fredrickson's."

She leaned in close when he spoke as though she were hard of hearing and slowly shook her head. "Don't recognize it. I live in San Francisco. There are a lot of wineries around here. I'd be glad to take you on a tour of my favorites sometime, if you'd like." She slipped a card between the pages of his book, traced her top lip with the tip of her tongue, and smiled seductively.

"That's very generous of you."

The baggage carousel started up with a loud clunk and the belt began to move. The woman inched forward, straining her neck for a view of the bags coming down the line. Adam's height was a bonus today as he could easily see over most of the heads crowding before him.

Five minutes later he snagged his green duffel bag and headed for the nearest exit. He glanced back. The woman was still searching for her luggage. She looked up, waggled her fingers at him, and mimicked the sign for *call me*.

Truthfully, he'd had quite enough of aggressive women in college. He wanted to be the pursuer, strike up a romance, and take a relationship to the next level. A woman who knew what she wanted was one thing, but pursuing a man with teeth and claws extended and a rope in hand was quite another. What ever happened to strong women that allowed their men to be stronger?

***

Margaret sat perfectly still at the kitchen counter, her hands gripping the edge, her bare feet propped on the spindles of the stool. She stared at the moving images on the muted television screen. Still wearing the cutoff sweatpants and tank top she'd thrown on when she got up that morning, she waited for the phone to ring. Handel promised to call as soon as he knew something. But although she glanced at the telephone every couple of minutes, willing a connection between her brother and herself, it didn't ring.

Since Davy left on the school bus that morning she'd spent the intervening hours scrubbing bathrooms, vacuuming, doing laundry, and basically keeping herself busy while she waited for Handel's call. Now, fresh out of chores and unwilling to work in the yard in case she missed hearing the ring, she waited, suspended between the present and the past…

Agosto Salvatore wasn't her first crush, but he was her first lover. Her only lover. She was fifteen when he came to live with his cousins Antonio and Carl Franzia, attending college during the day and waiting tables at his cousins' restaurant at night.

Carl and Handel had been on the football team together in high school and although they went separate ways through college, Handel to law school, Carl to a school of culinary art, they remained friends. After Handel and Margaret's mother died, Carl made a habit of showing up at their doorstep at least once a week with a huge container of Ravioli, Lasagna, or tortellini and a poor excuse for being in the area at suppertime with enough food to feed a Mormon family.

That summer the restaurant business took off and Carl couldn't leave as often as he would like, so he sent his cousin in his place. Agosto at twenty was darkly handsome, wise beyond his years, with worlds of experience oozing from his pores. Or at least that's how Margaret saw him. He was her ticket out of town, away from the pitying looks people cast her way because she'd lost both her parents; one to alcohol, the other to cancer.

Margaret knew she was pretty. She didn't flaunt it, but she didn't look in the mirror and dwell on imperfections either, as some girls were prone to do. She saw herself the way others did.

She had curves in all the right places, a wide mouth meant for kissing, high cheekbones and a pert nose. Her face framed by naturally blonde hair rivaled any California beach bunny. That was a lot of power to keep harnessed, especially at fifteen. But she managed to keep it reined in. Until Carl and Antonio's young cousin came to town.

When Agosto stood on her doorstep with a container of linguine and cream sauce, his dark eyes undressing her in the dim light of the porch, she didn't want to hold back. She wanted to let loose. She was an innocent, heat-seeking missile and he was a black hole pulling her in to her destruction. She lost part of herself forever in their time together. Despite her love for Davy, regret ran deep and painful in her soul.

She knew there were men out there with scruples, trustworthy men, honorable men, unlike Agosto, but she had yet to meet them. Only Handel held a place of esteem in her heart. Sometimes she was jealous of Billie Fredrickson for her relationship with Handel. But jealousy soon turned to guilt. Handel wanted a family of his own someday. He'd been a surrogate father to Davy for so long she didn't know what she'd do without him. On the other hand, she didn't want to stifle his dreams or hinder his chance at love. Even if it meant she and Davy move out and make it on their own.

It was time to prove she was more than a pretty face, the dumb blonde sister knocked up at fifteen. She may have gotten her high school diploma late and only succeeded in finishing a few college credits online, but she had skills. Given a chance she could...

The doorbell shook her from her reverie. She bolted off the stool, sending it tottering on two legs. She quickly righted it. The doorbell chimed again. She hurried to answer it. Who would stop by at this time of the afternoon? Other than the mailman with a package or Billie driving Davy home from the winery after dark, no one used the front door. The sound was always jolting, like an ambulance with the siren blaring suddenly in the road behind you.

She opened the door, her eyes slanted against the afternoon sun that poured through the screen. A man stood there, a duffel bag and leather guitar case propped against the porch railing, his hands jammed in the front pockets of a baggy pair of jeans. He stared across the south vineyard toward Fredrickson's winery.

"Can I help you?" she asked, keeping the screen door closed between them.

He was a stranger but something about his jaw line seemed familiar. His shaggy auburn hair glistened in the sun as though full of burning embers. When he turned to face her, surprise was evident in his expression. "This isn't Fredrickson's, is it," he said. He frowned and glanced down at a map folded in his hand.

"Nope." Margaret opened the screen to step out on the porch beside him. Harvest time was close and the almost overpowering sweetness of vine-ripened grapes mingled with the man's musky scent. His t-shirt was damp with perspiration along the neck and sleeves, and he smelled like Davy did when he came home from playing soccer after school. She glanced over his shoulder but didn't see a car in the driveway. She pointed across the field where he'd been staring moments before. "Fredrickson's is on the other side of that vineyard. You're almost there. Just another half mile down the road."

He groaned, reluctantly lifted his bags, and slipped the straps over his shoulders. "Half a mile, huh? Great." He blew out a breath of frustration. "It's my own fault. I should have called Billie for a ride, but I thought—hey, this is California, everyone hitches. Darned if I didn't have to walk the last ten miles. Apparently, folks around here are either leery of hitchhikers or they want to kill them. That was the most dangerous road I've ever walked on."

"You know Billie Fredrickson?" Margaret asked, shielding her eyes from the sun.

He nodded. "Sure. I've known her since I was a baby. She's my sister." His gaze abruptly left her face and traveled downward with blatant male appreciation, as though suddenly seeing her for the first time. He grinned and whistled through his front teeth. "I am definitely in California. Has anyone ever told you you're the spitting image of Marilyn Monroe?"

Margaret crossed her arms over her chest. It wasn't the first time she'd heard a man express appreciation of her resemblance to the Hollywood icon. In fact, in the past year it had been almost commonplace. So much so, that she contemplated dying her hair a dark shade of brown. But this time it didn't irk her—it angered her. Maybe because he was Billie's brother, or maybe because he was an immature, scruffy, smelly man, and she'd taken an instant dislike to him. Whatever the case, there wouldn't be any happy family get-togethers during the holidays if Handel married this jerk's sister.

"Gee, aren't you original. Your sister must be so proud." She snapped the screen open, stepped inside, and let it bang shut behind her before she closed and locked the front door.

***

"Terrific." Adam stared at the ancient two-story house. Billie would not be happy. He'd just offended one of her neighbors. Why couldn't he keep his mouth shut? A curtain fluttered at a side window and that was slammed shut too.

He let his gaze follow the curves and lines of the shuttered house looming before him. It was a pretentious farmer's shelter to say the least, the windows inset with ornamental framing, three chimneys rising collectively toward the sky, and a center tower that may once have held a bell, but was now enclosed. He shouldn't be surprised by the inhospitable reaction of the owner. Only a snob would live in a house with a bell tower.

He squinted up at the tower room. It did add an air of mystery to the structure. It probably had great acoustics too. Not to mention, the view from the windows would be amazing with a panorama of the valley and vineyards. He could imagine plugging in his guitar and jamming up there. He shook his head and turned away, retreating down the oak-lined driveway. That was something he'd never experience.

Adam picked up his pace when he heard the sound of an engine roaring to a stop at the end of the driveway. Maybe he could catch a ride. A school bus had pulled onto the shoulder of the road. The door opened. A young boy slowly hopped down the steps, one at a time, as though he had all afternoon.

"Hurry along, Davy. I haven't got all day." The driver scratched at his forehead where gray hair poked free of a baseball cap.

The boy took a leap and landed on the ground about five feet from the bus, a backpack clutched in one hand and a soccer ball in the other. He dropped the ball and waved. "Thanks for the ride, Mr. Hadley."

The driver grunted, pulled the door closed, and shifted into gear.

Adam picked up the dropped ball and bounced it from one thigh to another, tapped it with the side of his foot and sent it back to the boy. The kid dropped his book bag to catch the ball and stared in awe. "Cool! Are you a professional soccer player?" he asked, blonde hair hanging limply over his forehead and in his eyes. He combed it back with one hand and kicked the ball to Adam.

"Nope, but I played in college." He deftly kicked the ball up and bounced it from his head and back again. "It takes a lot of practice."

The boy bounced the ball off his head, but it flew too high and rolled along the driveway toward the house. "Sorry." He picked up his book bag and started running after the ball, then stopped and looked back. The tip of his tongue stuck out the corner of his mouth. "Hey, what were you doing at my house?" he asked. "Are you a friend of Uncle Handel's?"

The depth of Adam's stupidity hit him like a roller derby queen. Not only was Marilyn Monroe his sister's neighbor, she was also his sister's boyfriend's sister. That was a lot of sister problems. He shook his head.

"I'm Billie's brother, Adam. And you are?" he asked, already knowing the answer. The son of the woman who hated him.

"I'm Davy."

"Davy!" his mother called from the front porch, her voice sharp and forceful, not at all like the breathy movie star she resembled.

"I better go," Davy said, his grin contagious.

Adam grinned too. He watched Davy run toward the house and his waiting mom.

CHAPTER THREE

"I can't believe you're really here." Billie released Adam from a rib-crushing embrace. She motioned him into the house and watched as he hefted his bag. "You brought your guitar? You must be planning a long visit." Her brows drew together in a little frown.

Adam grinned to hide his uneasiness. "Sure, why not? I'm out of school, looking for my path in life. I might as well search in California as well as Minnesota."

"I thought you already had a job offer." The reprimand in her voice was obvious but instead of waiting for a reply she closed the door and led him through the house, down a hallway into a guest room.

A tall four-poster dwarfed the space, but the painting at the head of the bed immediately grabbed his attention. The surreal vision of vibrant colors fighting one another to dominate the canvas was almost more than he could take in. Billie was right when she told him her uncle was exorcising personal demons with his art.

"Uncle Jack's work?" He dropped the bags and stepped around his sister to get a better look. "I thought you auctioned them off or something."

She shrugged and lifted her chin. "I kept a couple. It seemed wrong to sell all of them. He was our uncle, after all. Besides, I see them in a different light now."

"Really? In a dark room with a dim flashlight?"

She smacked his shoulder. "Same little smart aleck you always were," she said, her voice light with laughter. "Are you hungry?"

He nodded and followed her to the kitchen.

"What did Mother say about you flying out here?" She pulled leftovers from the refrigerator; chicken breast, wild rice, and broccoli materialized from containers. She lifted a carton of milk. "Seems funny she didn't call me."

Adam scratched at the stubble along his cheek. "That's cause I didn't mention it to her."

She looked up from her preparations, amusement flickering in the depths of her eyes.

"She'd just try to talk me out of it. You know how she is."

Billie bit at her bottom lip, a longtime habit since she was a kid, and slipped the plate of food into the microwave. "Haven't learned how to deal with Mother yet without running away?" she asked. She turned to face him as they waited for the food to heat.

"Hey! I'm not the one who moved to California," he reminded her.

"I didn't move here to get away from Mother. That was a bonus." She smiled smugly.

"I'm going to tell her you said that," he threatened, and pulled his cell phone from his back pocket.

She laughed and shook her head, unafraid as ever. "No you won't. Cause then she'll know where you are."

"You're right. I'd rather be sucked into quicksand than have that conversation now. I'm too tired and hungry to deal with thirty questions." He sat at the butcher-block table, and propped his head on his hand. "You aren't going to quiz me, are you?"

"Not tonight," she said as she set the plate before him. "Maybe tomorrow." She watched him eat with obvious sibling affection.

He finished off the food in record time, leaned back in his chair with a sigh. "Thanks, that was great. You know, they don't feed people on planes anymore. And the shops in the airport are pure robbery."

"Did you take the taxi all the way out? It must have cost a fortune. Why didn't you call me?" she asked, her back to him as she rinsed his plate in the sink.

"Nope. I hitched—and walked a lot." He chuckled at the look of astonishment on her face. It reminded him of their mom. "Don't worry. I only met two serial killers and neither wanted me."

"It's no wonder."

"There's something else I should probably tell you though," he said. He stood to stretch the kinks from his back and deliberately avoided his sister's gaze by peering through the window of the back door. The yard was shadowed by the overhanging boughs of huge trees, edged by vineyards to the south. He tried to see through the foliage, toward the house he knew stood in the distance, but it was as remote as the woman who lived there.

Billie's groan was reminiscent of the Frankenstein monster in the movies they watched together as children. "Don't tell me. You've run away from home and Mom will be beating down the door shortly."

"Not exactly." Adam turned to face her. "I met your neighbor."

"Handel?"

He shook his head. "His sister. I knocked on her door by mistake. Thought it was the winery." He combed fingers through his hair, pushed it back from his forehead in a weary gesture. "You could have told me you lived by Marilyn Monroe reincarnated."

She groaned again, covered her mouth and released the breath of a laugh into her palm. "You didn't mention the resemblance to Margaret, did you?"

"Most women would be flattered," he muttered, annoyed by the teasing light in his sister's eyes. "She acted as if I likened her to a Guernsey cow rather than a sexy movie star. What's with women anyway?"

Billie cupped his scruffy chin in her hand as if he was still the little brother and not half a head taller than she. "Some women like to be admired for attributes other than big breasts and blonde hair. You might try looking below the surface."

He shrugged and pulled away. "That takes time," he said, moving toward the living room. "I didn't get the impression she gave guys like myself the opportunity to dig deeper. Is it just me or does she seem a bit stuck up to you too?"

Billie followed and plopped down on a leather sofa across from the recliner he stretched out in. "She has her reasons. I wouldn't call it stuck up; more like reserved. You would be too if everywhere you went men gaped and made lewd comments or catcalls."

"Beauty is such a curse." He wasn't usually so snide but he was tired and failed to keep it in. "And I didn't do any of those things," he argued, crossing his arms.

"I didn't say you did. But I'm sure that's what Margaret heard. She's been trying to live down her past for so long, she thinks everyone else is just as obsessed with it."

"At least Davy doesn't seem traumatized by her attitude." Adam yawned widely and rubbed a hand over his face.

"You met Davy?" His sister smiled, her whole face emanating warmth at mention of the kid. She apparently had fallen for more than one Parker male. "I don't think anything could traumatize that boy. He's the most secure child I've ever known. Margaret is a good mother. Davy is proof of that. She's not as confident as she wants people to believe and she comes off as brusque, often inhospitable, but underneath I think she just needs a friend."

"A friend, huh?"

"Yeah, a friend."

Her steady gaze was disconcerting and Adam couldn't help but look away. Friendship with a woman was seldom long-lived. If he liked them well enough to be friends, something physical was usually brewing on one side or the other. Platonic was not a word he could envision using in regard to the woman next door. He just wished there was some way to start over with Margaret Parker.

"So?" His sister's question brought him back to the conversation at hand.

"So, what?"

"So what are you really doing here? Besides ticking off my neighbor."

"Isn't it obvious?" He pulled his jean pockets inside out, revealing a ball of lent and twenty-six cents. "I need a job."

"You studied business and accounting," she said, frowning. "We need field workers right now. It's harvest time."

"I could try that—but someone told me your accountant is spending time in Sing Sing."

A smile lit up her eyes and she chuckled. "I was kind of hoping she got put out on Alcatraz."

"Good accountants are hard to find these days."

She pressed her lips together and looked away. "You don't have to tell me."

"Hey, I'm sorry. I didn't mean to bring up bad memories."

"It's okay." She slid her fingers over the smooth leather sofa, a shadow of pain in her eyes. "At least the bad memories are out in the open now. Believe me, they're much easier to deal with than nightmares."

"Are you doing the books yourself?"

"Right now I'm doing a bit of everything, but not mastering anything. Maybe new blood is a good idea. I could use the help."

"Terrific. When do I start?"

"Is tomorrow too soon?"

He grinned. "That gives me just enough time to press my three-piece suit."

"Lucky for you, we're a little more laid back around here. Suits are optional."

"Whew! That's a relief. Cause I didn't actually bring a suit."

She snorted. "I didn't actually believe you did."

***

Margaret set a plate of cheese and crackers on the floor beside her son where he hunched over a complicated Lego structure. He'd been working on it for the past four afternoons.

He looked up and smiled. "Thanks, Mom." His attention immediately returned to the task at hand. He was a natural at complicated directions and intricate details. Even at nine years old he seemed to have an innate sense of how things fitted together. She relied on him to direct her on any project that included boards, screws, or wrenches of any kind.

"What are you building there?" she asked, glancing about the room. The pile of socks and shorts she'd folded and left on the top of his dresser earlier was still there. She slid open the top drawer and placed them inside.

"It's a replica of the space station. I saw a picture on the Internet at school." He pushed a tiny block in place, his eyes narrowed into a squint. "But I'm not sure if this is right. I think I might have to print out a copy."

Margaret ruffled his hair. "You're something else." She headed for the door.

"Billie's brother is pretty cool, isn't he?" he said.

She stopped, one hand on the doorframe. "Why do you say that?"

"He's really good at soccer and he has a guitar. I bet he can play that rock and roll you like."

She tried not to laugh. "I think your cool meter is broken, babe. That guy was a jerk."

Davy narrowed his eyes as he considered her view. "Maybe he's like new wine. He just needs time to soak up the flavors around here and you'll like him better. I didn't know if I liked Billie when she first came and started living in Jack's house," he said, his voice thoughtful, " but now we're like best friends."

"Yeah? Well I didn't know about Billie right away either, but I'm pretty sure I won't change my mind about her brother."

He stared up at her a moment. "Don't you like men, Mom?" he said finally, his blue eyes intent.

The question struck her heart like an arrow. She didn't want Davy to think she was a man-hater, one of those women that put all of the male species into one box. He was, after all, becoming one of them. But lately she'd felt a growing tendency to blame everything wrong with her world upon the macho sex.

The rattle of the garage door brought her son to his feet. "Uncle Handel!" He ran past her, leaving the question still hanging unanswered in the room.

She followed him down the hall and into the kitchen where Handel stood before the open refrigerator, staring inside with a practiced eye. "What's for dinner?" he asked without turning around. He lifted the carton of orange juice and drank straight from the spout.

Beloved brother or not, Margaret wanted to throw herself at him and pummel him with her fists. Not because he was drinking from the carton like a pig, although that annoyed her too, but because he was acting as though this were any other day of the week. She'd waited patiently for his call all morning and afternoon, and he hadn't had the sense to pick up a phone. How could he walk in here and ask what's for dinner as though her whole world wasn't ready to fall apart? She knew him too well to think he'd actually forgotten to call. Something must have happened that he could only relate in person. So she continued to wait, her arms crossed tightly over her chest, jaw clenched in anticipation.

"Uncle Handel, guess what?" Davy interjected into the dark void of Margaret's thoughts.

Handel replaced the carton, let the door swing shut, and slowly turned toward them. Margaret saw his face change from somber to pleasantly cheerful, obviously for Davy's benefit. Was that pity she detected in his eyes when he glanced her way? It was hard to say. Her brother was usually very adept at hiding his feelings. After all, he was a lawyer.

"Do I have to? I had a really long day, Kid. Guessing takes energy, and I'm all out." He slumped playfully against the refrigerator as though he could barely stand upright.

Davy grabbed Handel's arm and pulled him toward the kitchen table. "Sit down and I'll tell you."

"All right."

Margaret went to the refrigerator and pulled out the package of hamburger patties she'd planned to cook for dinner. Thoughts of what may have transpired between Handel and Agosto blocked out Davy's conversation at the table. Until Adam Fredrickson's name came up.

"He had a guitar on his back while he was kicking the ball. Can you believe it? It was cool!"

Handel met Margaret's eye. "Is that right? Billie's brother showed up? I didn't even know she was expecting him," he said, clearly disappointed that he was out of the loop.

Margaret plopped the burgers onto the preheated skillet and set on a lid. "I don't think she knew either. I'm pretty sure he conceived the idea for this grand visit on his own."

Handel's eyes narrowed at her tone, but he didn't comment.

So predictable, she thought. He never caused waves. He certainly wouldn't be first in a pool of criticism that involved his girlfriend's brother. Chalk up another point for the male brotherhood. She poured a package of frozen corn into a bowl and set it to cook in the microwave. When she looked up he was still watching her, a sad expression on his face.

"Uncle Handel, do you want to see my space station?"

"Sure." He followed Davy down the hallway.

Alone, Margaret couldn't keep her thoughts from Agosto, and the reason for his return to California. Davy. Her son would not be a pawn in the hands of that bastard. She wouldn't allow it. Handel promised, and she knew his word was as solid as Gibraltar. So what wasn't he telling her?

Davy's laughter echoed through the house and she smiled, listening. He was her world; why she got up in the morning. She couldn't lose him. She turned back to the stove and flipped the burgers, her hands shaking with the effort.

"Are you all right?" Handel appeared in the doorway alone.

"What do you think? I've been waiting all day for you to call." She hated the antagonistic sound of her voice, but it's what she felt. Waiting was not one of her strong points.

"Sorry. I wanted to talk to you in person." He slumped onto a stool at the counter, but remained silent.

She wiped her hands on the dishtowel. "So how was he?" she asked in a quiet voice.

"Same obnoxious little… Davy! I thought you were going to work on your space station for a while, buddy."

Davy stood at Handel's elbow. "I'm tired of that. I wanted to talk to you." His expression was openly curious as though he knew he'd come in at an interesting moment. "Who are you talking about?" he asked.

"Nobody," Margaret said too quickly to be convincing. He was an intelligent boy and more observant than she often gave him credit for. Deflecting the question would probably make him more interested in the answer. But right now she couldn't deal with the questions that would be sure to follow. Instead she turned away, pretending dinner preparations had her full attention. "Are you hungry? The burgers are almost ready. Set the table for me, kiddo."

CHAPTER FOUR

Billie led and he followed. Just like when they were kids. Through the neighbor's hedge or cross-country to California, she was always one step ahead. He trailed her now through the door of the winery and down a sun-brightened hallway. She stopped at an open office door and stepped inside, pulling him along with a tug on his jacket sleeve. A youngish woman occupied the desk, glasses pushed up on her forehead, squinting at a computer screen. Her hair was redder than his own, a flaming bob atop petite features.

"Morning, Sally. This is my brother, Adam. He's going to check out the books for me. Could you give him access to the computer and whatever he needs? I've got to talk to Mario, but I'll be right back." She winked in his direction and hurried out the door.

Sally cleared her throat, eyes wide with interest. "So you're Adam," she drawled in a teasing tone, as though she'd heard more about him than he'd wish to share.

Had Billie brought up the time his junior high girl friend mowed him down with her bicycle after he broke up with her? Or that he got pummeled with tomatoes during his performance of Hamlet in the school play? "Yep, that's me."

She stood up and thrust out a hand. "Welcome to Fredrickson's. I suppose I can count on you not to cook the books or try to murder your sister."

He shrugged. "I promise not to cook the books, but I can only give you a definite maybe on the murder thing. One day at a time."

She grinned. "Good enough for me."

"So where do you want me?"

The office had two terminals set up, one on Sally's desk, the other on a card table in the corner of the room. She dipped her head toward the latter. A metal folding chair awaited him. He could already imagine his rear end going numb.

"Don't look so glum, little brother," Billie said as she breezed back in. "It's only temporary. You can have the extra office down the hall as soon as the computer tech gets the wiring set up. He'll be here tomorrow."

Adam pulled out the chair and sat. The screen was black. "Got a password for this thing?"

"FredricksonWinery," Billie and Sally said, nearly in unison.

He raised his eyebrows. "Original. No one would ever think of that."

"Don't be so sarcastic. You probably couldn't come up with anything better. Besides, why would anyone want to break into our computer system?" Billie said, pulling out a file drawer and rifling through a folder.

"I don't know. Why would some crazy accountant woman try to kill you? Strange things happen in your vicinity."

A giggle escaped Sally's lips and Billie glared. "Don't encourage him."

The phone rang. Sally picked it up. "Yep. She's right here," she said after a minute and held out the phone. "It's for you, boss."

Billie took the phone out into the hall. Her voice was muffled but she sounded disappointed. Sally shuffled past him to get a cup of water from the cooler by the door.

"Hear anything interesting?" he asked.

"She's talking to Handel," she said, before realizing he was teasing her. She gave him a wry smile. "Sorry. Bad habit. But how else am I supposed to know what's going on around here?"

Billie stepped around the corner and held out the phone. "If it's any of your business, I'll be sure and let you know."

"If you say so." Sally returned the phone to her desk and leaned over Adam's shoulder, her hands on the keyboard. "Here. Let me get you into the books."

Adam glanced at Billie. "If you've got things to do, go ahead. Don't feel as though you have to hang around and take care of me."

"Believe me, I have no such feelings. This is the busiest time of year for the winery and I have lots to do. Besides, you seem to be well taken care of. So, see ya!" She waved a hand as she walked out without showing an ounce of remorse.

He straightened and nearly bumped heads with Sally, still hovering over his left shoulder. "Sorry."

She pressed her face close to his ear and inhaled deeply. "Hmm, fresh Minnesota country boy. I could just eat you up."

He jerked back so fast the metal chair nearly tipped over.

Sally exploded in laughter and dropped back into her desk chair. "You should see your face! Where's a hidden camera when you need one?" she hooted.

"That wasn't funny," he mumbled, his face hot with embarrassment. He readjusted the chair and faced the computer screen. "What kind of a wacky place does my sister run here anyway?"

She continued to chuckle intermittently even while she typed. "We have to do something for fun. Watching grapes ferment is a pretty boring pastime."

When he didn't respond, she expelled loudly. "All right, I'm sorry kid. I shouldn't have teased you. But I didn't know Midwesterners were so touchy."

He scraped his chair around to face her. "We are not touchy. We are reserved," he said in a voice typical of his mother. "That type of behavior in the workplace may be called teasing in California. In Minnesota they call it sexual harassment. Ask Billie. I'm sure she dealt with cases all the time."

"Are you going to turn me in?" Her smile deepened.

"Don't tempt me."

***

"So what's the verdict?"

Adam looked up from the screen. His sister stood in the doorway and Sally was no where in sight. The clock on the wall said it was well past lunch, or maybe that was his growling stomach talking. He stood up and stretched the kinks out of his back.

"You definitely need to make some changes around here. And soon. You can't remain solvent if you're putting out more than you're bringing in. Cutting back on employees may be a short-term option, but by next year if things haven't picked up..." he let the thought hang.

Billie glanced quickly down the hallway and stepped inside shutting the door. "Don't say that so loud. I don't want to spook my people. I can't let anyone go. We're already down to a skeleton crew. The grapes are ready to be harvested and the tasting room is flooded with tourists. I can't afford to close that down during Crush because we really need the income, but I need everyone's focus on bringing in our crop. I'll think of something. I have to think of something."

"If Mom knew you were struggling --

"I'm not asking her for a loan. That's out of the question. Do you know how much leverage she would have over my life if I did?"

The look of panic on her face made him laugh. "Don't worry. I'm not calling her. I just thought it would be easier than going to a bank. She did make a killing last year on that Google stock. I still can't believe I missed my chance." He shook his head.

"It takes money to make money, and you didn't have any to begin with."

"True."

"Hungry? I'll take you out for lunch." She swung the door back open.

"Are you sure you can afford it?"

"No, but Handel can. He invited us to meet him at Herbies at two."

He shut down the programs he was working on and followed her out the door. He was disappointed that Fredrickson Winery was floundering. He'd pinned his hopes on staying awhile, working for his sister, maybe getting some music gigs in the city at night. He'd heard there were lots of clubs and places for a musician to play if they had the right stuff. He was pretty sure he did, he only needed a captive audience to prove it.

Billie didn't talk much on the way to the restaurant. She bit at her bottom lip and seemed engrossed in thoughts she wasn't ready to share. He stared out the window at the vineyards they passed and thought about what he was going to do now. He couldn't ask her to pay him a salary if she couldn't afford the staff she already had. He'd just have to look for a job elsewhere.

Herbies bar and grill had a replica of Disney's lovable old VW Beetle parked in the middle of the restaurant. Some kids had climbed in and sat grinning while their mother took their picture. A knockoff rendition of *Rocking around the Clock* poured out from overhead speakers, nearly drowned out by the full lunch crowd.

Billie glanced around the restaurant, eagerly seeking the man they were to meet. Her face lit up and she waved. "There he is."

Adam followed her across the room, dodging tables and waiters. He'd been the only man in his sister's life for a long time and although she looked happier than he'd ever seen her, he felt strangely over-protective. He hoped he wasn't turning into a male version of his mother.

Handel stood and kissed Billie then reached past her and shook hands with Adam. "It's good to finally meet you, Adam." He inclined his head toward the woman still seated in a corner of the booth. "This is my sister, Margaret. I believe you've already met."

Margaret's welcoming smile couldn't have been colder if chipped from an iceberg. She lifted her cup of coffee and took a sip, dismissing him as soon as she'd laid eyes on him.

Adam waited for Billie to scoot in next to Handel before taking the remaining seat next to the Ice Queen. He wondered if he'd come down with a case of freezer burn if he got too close. The booth was narrow and his arm grazed hers as he settled in. She pulled back as though he carried the plague, and slid closer toward the wall on her side.

Handel and Billie didn't seem to notice. They were too busy looking into each other's eyes as though they'd been apart for months rather than mere hours. He glanced away and hoped the waiter came quickly to take their orders.

"So, you showed up yesterday and Billie already put you to work, huh?" Handel said.

"Something like that."

Billie smiled. "Adam is a whiz at numbers, he has an accounting degree, and he can even play a mean guitar."

He heard a distinct sigh of boredom from the woman beside him. He turned toward her. "So what do you do, Margaret?" he asked. "Besides, telling men exactly *where to go* when they stop and ask directions?"

Handel coughed and raised his glass to his lips to cover a grin. Billie was turning a lovely shade of pink and looked like she wanted to punch him in the arm again. Just like old times.

Margaret set her glass down but held his gaze. "Sometimes I help them on their way."

Providentially, the waiter showed up at that moment and encouraged everyone to order the special of the day—the Herbie Burger. When the waiter left, Handel quickly picked up the conversation.

"How long are you planning to stay, Adam? We should take you out on the town some night. It's always fun to listen to the street musicians or attend a concert in the park."

"That would be great, but I'm not really sure what my plans are at this point."

"What do you mean—you don't know?" Billie said, "I thought you were..."

"I changed my mind." He shrugged. "San Francisco is calling my name. Thought I'd answer the call and do a little walk-about."

"Figures," Margaret said, her voice like a jab to his ribs.

Why did this woman's opinion of him matter? He didn't know her from—Eve. When it came to men, Margaret Parker was a cynical shrew. She thought all men were the same and he obviously just confirmed her belief pattern.

"Sorry to disappoint you, but Billie is struggling with the winery and I'm afraid I'd be dead weight around here. She needs someone with expertise at running a winery, not just a number cruncher."

"That's not true, Adam." Billie said, leaning forward, her hands on the table. "You can help me in many more ways than crunching numbers. You're better at problem solving and coming up with ideas. That's what I need right now. Someone with ideas for change. Cause what we're doing is obviously not working. And don't worry, I have plenty of hard labor for you when the numbers run out."

"I thought the *Time in a Bottle* brand was selling well," Handel said, his gaze narrowed on Billie. He covered her hand with his. "Has something else happened since we talked?"

"No. Only the same old thing. It took Adam pointing it out to me this morning that made me see I can't live off of my uncle's wishful thinking, and neither can my employees. Making Fredrickson's profitable again may be a pipedream."

"You've got to give it time. It can take months, even years, to get your brand out there."

"We don't have years. I'm not sure we even have months. I haven't got enough savings to prop us up that long."

Handel put his arm around her shoulders and pulled her close. "You know I'll help anyway I can."

She nodded. "I know, but you have your own practice to worry about. What I need is someone with winery experience, fresh money-saving ideas, awesome management skills, winemaking expertise, and a willingness to work for next to nothing."

Margaret cleared her throat, "I have…" she started, but the waiter brought their platters and she fell silent. Adam glanced her way. She seemed nervous, unwrapping her flatware and placing the paper napkin on her lap. She kept her head down, avoiding his gaze.

Billie glanced around at their glum faces after the waiter left. "Wow. I sure know how to shut down a party, don't I? Don't let me ruin your Herbie burgers." She picked up a fry and dipped it in ketchup.

Adam eyed his burger suspiciously. Back home, a California burger usually had tomato, lettuce, and mayo, but this one had sprouts poking out the sides. He took the top bun off to dissect the innards. Besides sprouts, he found sliced green olives and some kind of unknown sauce, two of his least favorite things. He proceeded to scrap the meat patty with his knife.

"Don't like our local cuisine?" Margaret asked from her quiet corner.

"Not especially. I'm more of a pizza and tacos kind of guy." He plopped the top bun back down and picked up the burger. "But I'll eat most anything."

Billie laughed. "Yeah, sure. You'll eat anything Mom cooks or a fast food restaurant serves up in paper wrappers—but anything? I don't think so."

"I'm not picky. I'm discerning." He took a big bite to end the critique of his personal tastes.

"So how's Davy doing in school this year, Margaret?" Billie asked, switching gears. "I haven't seen him around much lately."

"He puts up with it." Margaret smiled, her face lighting up. "Obviously he only attends class so he can play on the soccer team. He's bouncing that silly ball off his head every time I turn around."

"Or building some crazy structure with Legos," Handel added. "I think he's going to be a wine-making, soccer playing, architect."

"Those are quite diverse interests," Adam said, and took another bite of his burger.

"Well, some of the male species actually use their brains as well as their brawn."

With his mouth full he couldn't very well respond, and perhaps that's what she counted on. Billie caught his eye and intuited a warning to tread lightly. As if he was the instigator.

"Davy is really an apt pupil. He's learning winemaking faster than I thought possible. Sometimes I feel like he's teaching me rather than the other way round," Billie said.

Margaret nervously played with the napkin in her lap again. "That's probably because he's been around the winery his whole life. I worked there too when I was growing up. You learn a lot just from observing, you know."

Why did talk of the winery make her nervous? Adam watched her between bites, trying not to look as though he was staring. Was she still traumatized by her father's return and the revelations that led to his subsequent arrest? He couldn't imagine learning that his father was a child molester. He decided to cut her a little slack. She was human after all, even if she did look like a goddess.

Adam took another bite of burger. He'd scraped off most of the strange ingredients and it was actually pretty good now. He dipped a fry in ketchup and poked it in his mouth too. He glanced out the window at clear blue skies. "Doesn't it ever rain around here? It was pouring when I left Minneapolis yesterday. Not that I miss it, but it looks kind of dry here."

Margaret sent him a scathing glare that may have meant she thought his question was totally stupid or she just didn't like the sound of his voice. "Rain we can do without. It would damage the wine berry crop during Crush. One bad season and a winegrower…" She stopped.

"Could be out of business," Billie finished, her voice soft with worry.

"I thought rain was good for crops."

"Not when they're ripe. It can cause them to rot."

They finished eating while making small talk, bordering on tiny talk. When the waiter cleared the dishes and brought the check, everyone was eager to go. There wasn't a mad rush to the door, but it was a definite beeline. Adam refrained from speaking, afraid he'd just say the wrong thing again and set Ms. Ice Queen off on a rant. He didn't know why she seemed to dislike him so much. He thought he was a pretty likable guy, all things considered.

Handel put his arm around Billie as they walked across the parking lot. He whispered something in her ear and she laughed. Margaret and Adam walked a few steps behind. He felt like he used to when his mom made him go along as chaperone on his sister's dates.

Handel stopped beside a red Porsche and opened the passenger door. "Could you drive Margaret back? I need to speak with your sister and Margaret needs to be home when Davy gets off the bus."

Billie tossed her keys and Adam caught them. She smiled. "I really appreciate it. "

Without waiting for confirmation she slid into the glove leather seat and Handel closed the door. He moved quickly around the car to the driver's side and slid behind the wheel. When the engine purred to life, he gave them a thumbs-up before pulling out onto the street.

Adam heard Margaret let out a frustrated breath and turned around. He was nearly blinded by the look in her eyes. "Whoa!" He made the sign of the cross, warding off evil. "I hope that isn't meant for me cause I had nothing to do with this. Your brother left you high and dry. I'm the kind stranger seeing you home."

"I don't need anyone to see me home. I'm not a child."

"I never thought you were. In fact, you look pretty grown up to me."

She glanced away and shook her head in disgust, but he noticed a slight shade of pink stain her cheeks.

"What have I done to tick you off? You don't even know me, but you've been sending me a definite signal that if I got hit by a bus you wouldn't mourn my passing."

Her lips turned up slightly at that. "Sorry. You're right. I don't know you and you don't know me. Let's leave it at that, shall we?"

He shrugged. "All right. Do you want a ride? I happen to be heading that direction anyway."

"Thanks. That would be fine."

She followed him to the car, but when he moved to open her door she waved him off. He got in and turned the key in the ignition. She slid in beside him, not saying a word. They moved out into traffic and she directed him back to the highway toward Fredrickson's. The radio was set to an oldies station and he sang along, ignoring her, as she seemed to desire.

They flew past vineyards that all looked much the same to him. He hoped she'd let him know when it was time to turn. Finally he chanced a glance in her direction. She stared straight ahead.

"Can I ask you a question?"

She sighed and crossed her arms over her chest. "If you must."

"What were you going to ask my sister back there?"

She looked at him with a spark of surprise before she dropped her gaze. "What are you talking about?"

"You know what I'm talking about. She said she needed a manager and you started to say something. Why'd you stop?"

"That's two questions. Did you want to know what I was going to say, or why I stopped?"

He shook his head. "Wow. You are a piece of work."

She angled her body toward him, her arm across the back of the seat. "Now you're just being obtuse."

"I'm insensitive?"

She shrugged.

He turned up the radio. The heavy rock beat of *Barracuda* thumped through the speakers.

She flipped it back off, not ready to drop the subject. "I've lived by the winery my whole life. I worked there. I learned the winemaking process from your uncle when I was a child, just like Davy is doing now. I hung out and watched Jack managing the place, overseeing the vineyards. He let me be involved, explained what was going on." She paused. "Up until I had Davy. But I've read and kept up on things, talked with other vintners that stopped by. I have my own vines and make my own wine. I know how to run a winery. I have money saving ideas your sister could employ. I have experience that isn't from books, but from life, and just because I'm a woman without a college degree doesn't mean I'm not qualified."

Her sudden tirade felt personal but he knew it wasn't. She'd been too insecure to put it all out there in front of Billie, but for some reason had no problem blasting him with her "I am woman" speech. He kept his eyes on the road. "Sounds like you're the one with the skewed perception. If you think you can do the job then why didn't you say so? You really believe Billie would take you less seriously because you're a woman?" he gave a derisive snort. "That's a cop out."

"I don't want her to hire me just because I'm Handel's sister," she admitted, her voice suddenly subdued.

He glanced across at her and back to the road, slightly offended. "You mean the way she hired me just because I'm her brother?"

"I didn't mean it that way. I'm sure you're a perfectly adequate accountant. But that's part-time work. Fredrickson's needs a full-time manager and chief winemaker. Someone who knows wine. Someone who knows Fredrickson's."

He pulled off the highway and followed the gravel drive leading up to her house. A long black limousine stretched in the shade of a huge oak beside the Parker home, windows reflecting the glint of afternoon sun. A chauffeur immediately climbed out from behind the wheel and reached to open the back door for whoever waited inside.

Adam sensed Margaret's mood change at sight of the strange vehicle. He pulled the car in behind the limo and shut off the ignition. A man slowly stepped out of the open door, straightened his suit coat and glanced their way. Margaret's sharp intake of breath was more than surprise—it sounded like fear to Adam. He looked her way. She'd gone pale beneath her tan, and the fiery spark had left her eyes.

"Damn him," she muttered, her lips barely moving.

"Who is he?" Adam asked.

She didn't answer or move to get out, but appeared frozen in place.

Adam opened his door and stepped out. "Can I help you with something?" he asked, taking an immediate dislike to the stranger. He was a greased, primped, coiffed, pedicured kind of man—the kind Hollywood used in place of real men. The kind women were lured in by, like a moth to a bug-zapper.

The man stared at him for a moment as though assessing his importance, then his lips turned up derisively. "I think not. I'm here to see Margaret," he said, with a foreign accent. He tried to go around him but Adam blocked his way.

"I don't think Margaret wants to see you."

The man stopped midstride and glared up at him. "I don't think this is any of your business. Get out of my way."

Adam smiled. He would enjoy tossing the pompous little greased monkey back in his limo and sending him on his way. But before he made a move, the car door opened behind him.

"It's all right, Adam. I'll take care of this. Go home."

"Yes, go home, Adam," the man repeated, a smirk lifting his lips and lighting his dark eyes.

Adam ignored the jibe and turned around. Margaret's face was set, but there was something he couldn't ignore. No matter what she said, she was afraid to be alone with this guy. She might use it as an excuse to continue hating on him, but he wouldn't leave her with this jerk even if she begged him.

"You said you were going to show me the tower, remember?" he said, throwing the lie out there like a buoy.

Her eyes clung to his, seizing the lifeline.

He smiled, leaned against the front of the car and folded his arms over his chest. "I'll wait."

The man looked as though he wanted to clamp his teeth down on Adam's ankle like an inbred poodle, but instead he slipped a cigarette between his lips and lit it with the flick of a lighter. He took a drag before smiling at Margaret again, the smarmy charm back in place after sucking on his nicotine crutch. "Margaret. You're more beautiful than I remember," he said, as she slowly approached him.

"What do you want? I told you when you left, I didn't ever want to see you again."

He laughed softly and spread his hands. "That was a long time ago. We were both children. We didn't know what we were saying."

"I'm pretty sure you knew exactly what you were saying, Agosto—in English and Italian. But if I wasn't clear back then, let me clarify now. I want you to leave my property and never set foot on it again."

"You always called me August. I love the way my Americanized name sounds on your lips." He reached out and she drew sharply back.

"Don't touch me!"

"I only wanted…"

"I don't care what you want. You gave up your rights a long time ago and there's no going back." She brushed past him and ran up the steps to the front door.

He made as though to follow, but Adam pulled away from the car and grabbed his arm. "I wouldn't go there if I were you."

The man jerked away, his face red and angry. "If you put a hand on me again…" he spit out, pointing his finger in Adam's face.

Adam raised his brows. "What?"

The man swore under his breath, strode to the limo and yanked the door open. He turned to look up at the house, but Margaret had already gone inside. He climbed in and slammed the door. The big car slowly pulled away.

Adam waited until it disappeared down the highway before walking up to the house and knocking. She didn't answer. He waited a couple more minutes and then turned to leave.

Halfway to the car, he heard the door open behind him. He turned and looked up at the house. She pushed open the screen door, a squeak of rusty hinges inviting him in. "I thought you wanted to see the tower," she said.

CHAPTER FIVE

Agosto slouched in the seat, puffing on his cigarette. Anger spread through him, burning his stomach with acid. He stared out the window, replaying the scene. He was sure that if that young man hadn't been there Margaret would have listened. He knew she still cared, that he was never out of her thoughts. How could he be? She was raising his son, after all.

They passed a school bus dropping off children along the highway. He sat up straighter and turned to watch as two young kids ran down the driveway to their home before the bus pulled back onto the highway.

"Go back," he ordered the driver.

It was another half mile down the road before the driver found a spot large enough to turn around in. He caught up to the school bus a few minutes later, as it stopped at the Parker's drive.

"Pull over," Agosto ordered.

The limo slowed and pulled onto the gravel shoulder of the road, a safe distance behind the bus. Agosto watched the bus doors flip open. It seemed like eons before a young, tow-headed boy jumped to the ground and turned to look up at the driver. He waved before the doors of the bus closed. The boy dropped a soccer ball and kicked it toward the house, then ran after it to kick it again. He soon disappeared around the curve of the driveway, blocked from view by gnarly old olive trees growing thick along the road.

Agosto leaned back against the seat and smiled. He had a son. It had never been so real to him before, but now that he'd seen the boy…he felt a sense of pride, of accomplishment. He had sired a son and the boy was the spitting image of him. Granted, he had his mother's blonde hair, but everything else was straight from the Salvatore bloodline. He chuckled and ran his fingers through his hair. Margaret couldn't have gotten over him. She'd seen him in their son's face for the past nine years.

"Take me back to the hotel," he told the driver. He closed his eyes and imagined what it would be like when he bedded Margaret once again. She was more beautiful and curvaceous than he remembered. She'd matured into a spirited woman. There was fire in her eyes now—a wild, free spirit. He would enjoy breaking and molding her to his will. And she would enjoy the ride. He would allow her to come to Italy with them if she cooperated. She would probably expect marriage and perhaps he would concede. After all, his father would wish his grandson to be legitimate before he wrote him into the will. But it wasn't absolutely necessary.

***

"This is some view you've got up here." Adam moved through the doorway and across the empty room to stand at the curve of glass and gaze out over the countryside. Vineyards, lush and green, stretched for miles, punctuated by clumps of olive trees here and there. Men were at work in the fields, the Fredrickson's red pickup truck parked between vineyards on a stretch of gravel road that followed the property line. Winding off in the distance was the snakelike curve of a manmade canal.

He turned slowly to look back toward the highway and saw the school bus pulling up at the end of the drive. He watched Margaret's son, Davy, hop down the steps, blonde hair flopping over his forehead.

"Looks like Ernesto has the men checking the grapes. They have to get the crop in at the exact right time," Margaret explained, still gazing out at Fredrickson's fields.

The bus pulled away and Davy kicked his ball toward the house. Adam's gaze shifted a few degrees to the right. A hundred yards or so down the road, partially obscured by a tangle of olive trees, a long black limo was parked on the gravel shoulder. Davy was already up to the house before the limo slid into the end of the driveway, turned around and sped back toward town.

"So who was that obnoxious foreigner anyway?" Adam asked, suddenly very curious and a bit concerned. Why would the man sneak back and then leave again? Was he waiting to catch Margaret alone, or...

"No one important."

She still stared out the window in the direction of the men, her lips pressed into a thin line of resolve. He pushed his hands in the back pockets of his jeans and watched her. She was definitely a hardheaded woman. "Not important, huh? Well he obviously thinks he is. He came back."

"What?" She crossed to stand at his side, staring toward the road.

He pointed. "His limo was out there on the shoulder of the highway. After Davy got off the bus and walked up to the house, they drove off."

Her eyes widened and then narrowed in anger. "Why didn't you tell me?" She pushed past him and hurried through the door and down the stairs, her feet clattering against the wooden treads all the way to the ground floor. Apparently the man in the limo was more important to Margaret than she let on.

"Davy!" she called out, her voice muffled but clearly worried. The bang of the back door reverberated.

He turned and stared across the vineyards, not really seeing the beauty of the land but feeling frustrated beyond words. He thought he was making a little headway, but it seemed he flunked her man test once again. He wondered how the fancy-suited Italian came out on her scale of 1-10. That man had her full attention even when he'd already disappeared.

"Are you planning on camping out up there," Margaret called from the bottom of the stairs a few minutes later, "or would you like some coffee?"

A slow smile turned up the corners of his mouth. Maybe he'd gotten a passing grade after all. He moved through the door. "On my way," he called down the stairs.

He followed the fresh-brewed coffee smell through the house to the kitchen. Country white cupboards with glass panes encircled granite countertops and stainless steel appliances. Davy sat on a stool at the counter eating apple slices with peanut butter. The boy turned around and grinned, his mouth oozing juice. "Hey! You're Billie's brother."

"That I am. It would probably be easier if you just called me Adam though. Billie's brother is kind of long and doesn't really have the same flare."

Margaret motioned for him to sit down at the table. "Do you take cream or sugar?" she asked, filling two red 49er mugs from a thermal carafe.

"Black is fine," he said, still not a big coffee lover but unwilling to admit it when she was offering this tentative hand of friendship.

She handed him a mug of steaming coffee and sat across from him, wrapping her fingers around her mug. "So, why did you really come here?"

He blew out the breath of a laugh. "You don't make small talk, do you?

She shrugged and sipped her coffee, waiting.

"I have an accounting degree, but I really want to play my music. I hoped that maybe here I could do both."

"What kind of music do you play?" she asked, the hint of a smile lighting her eyes.

"I play a little jazz and classical, but I formed my calluses on rock and roll."

"Yes!" Davy yelled, pumping his arm. "I knew it."

"Davy…" his mother sent him a withering look and he went back to eating his fruit.

"So what do *you* want to be when you grow up?" he asked.

"I've wanted to be a wine vintner since I was ten. Jack told me I could work for him when I got out of high school but," she glanced at Davy, "life happened. I've taken some college courses online for business and agriculture but I think experience is most important in this business."

"I'm sure you're right. I know absolutely nothing about wine or grapes, except that I like them. I want to be able to help Billie, but I don't know what I can do."

"That's no reason to run off. You should stay and support her and do whatever she asks you to. Even a green-behind-the-ears accountant should be able to help with the Crush."

"Crush? I keep hearing that. You mean, walking on the grapes?"

She grinned. "Crush is another word for harvest. We bring in the grapes and crush them for wine. It's a time for hard work and celebration. Everybody pitches in at a small winery like Fredrickson's."

"Will you be there too?"

"I usually come and help out. But I have my own grapes to harvest as well. Enough to keep me fairly busy for a time."

"Mom lets me help," Davy said.

"I bet you're good at it."

"Yep!"

"I guess you two have a mutual admiration society going on. Davy seems to think you're an extraordinary soccer player."

He grinned over at Davy who was turned around on his stool, watching them. "Extraordinary? I don't think so. I'm a passable soccer player. Good enough to play more than I sat on the bench in college, but nothing special."

Margaret raised her brows, obviously amused. "That's not what I heard."

"Yeah! You bounced the ball off your head and knees just like those guys on TV." Davy jumped down from his perch to go through the motions. He looked like a miniature mime without the white makeup. "Want me to get the ball so you can show Mom your cool moves?" he offered.

Margaret burst out laughing and then clamped a hand over her mouth as though to stance the flow, but her eyes continued to sparkle with mirth.

Adam shook his head. "No thanks. I think she gets the picture."

"Are you staying for dinner?"

"Davy! What have I told you…" she began.

"Not to invite people without talking to you first? But you're right here… so can he?"

Adam loved seeing the pink color stain her cheeks, but he didn't want to overstay his welcome, so he let her off the hook. "I have to get back to the winery. Billie had me doing some bookwork and I never really finished. But thanks for the invitation," he said, rising from his chair. He met Margaret's surprised look with a smile. "Maybe you'll give me a raincheck?"

"What's that mean?" Davy asked.

"It means that Adam is welcome to come for dinner tomorrow night if he's available," she said, not looking away.

"I'd love to." Adam moved to put his nearly full cup in the sink. "Thanks for the coffee and for showing me the view."

Outside on the steps, he turned and took one more look at the beautiful woman standing inside the screen door, her son beside her. "See you tomorrow night then."

She nodded.

As he opened the car door and slid into the seat he heard Davy say, "Oh shoot! Tomorrow I'm going to the winery to work with Billie after school and she's making tacos for dinner."

"So? You love tacos," he heard Margaret say, before they moved away from the door and out of his hearing.

He twisted the key in the ignition and the engine revved to life. It felt like his heart restarted as well. He pulled the door closed and slipped the car into reverse. She'd known full well they would be dining alone tomorrow. He imagined she didn't do anything without thinking it through. He wasn't sure how that made him feel. Lucky or leery? Maybe a little of both. She was a complicated woman. But he couldn't help smiling as he pulled onto the highway and drove the half mile down the road to Fredrickson's.

***

"Where have you been all afternoon?" Adam demanded when his sister strolled leisurely into the office a quarter after six. Sally had already left for the day and other than the cleanup crew in the tasting room, he assumed he was the only one still working.

She looked a little too happy to have spent the last hours discussing her failing business with Handel. She didn't reply, but dropped her purse on Sally's desk and flopped down in the swivel chair, a grin stretching her lips like a Cheshire cat—or like a cat that ate a canary—he wasn't sure which.

"So you've got nothing to say after deserting me at that restaurant with a woman who clearly abhorred me and running off with your boyfriend like a teenager in heat?"

"Sorry," she said, not looking sorry at all. "I meant to be back earlier, but you know…" She held her hand out toward him and waggled her fingers, loaded down by a diamond ring that sparkled wickedly in the fluorescent office light.

"What the…?"

"My sentiments exactly," Sally said, bursting through the door and grabbing Billie's hand to stare at the rock on her finger. "I can't believe Handel finally popped the question. It's been long enough!"

"Where did you come from?" he asked, "I thought you went home."

"Thanks for your invaluable vigilance, newbie, but I was just in back talking to Loren and picking up a bottle of wine for my date." Sure enough she held a bottle of Fredrickson's against her chest with one arm while clinging to his sister's hand with the other.

He rescued it from her and set it carefully on the desk. With both arms free, she threw them around Billie and hugged her tight, mooning over the ring like it was the first engagement diamond she'd ever seen.

"It's beautiful! Did he get down on one knee? Did you make him beg? Was it the most romantic moment of your life?"

The rapid-fire questions seemed to take his sister aback. She continued to grin, wordlessly.

"Hey, slow down there, red. Can't you see Billie's not firing on all cylinders? As a divorce attorney, I'm sure this whole marriage thing has her tied up in knots. One of them must be shutting off her voice box."

Billie scowled at him while managing to extricate herself from Sally's clutches. She stood up and gently pushed her over excited friend away. "Handel's proposal was probably everything you've ever dreamed of. I'll leave it at that."

Her cryptic reply only made Sally more curious. "What? No details?"

"What's the deal with you romance types? You get all twittery when a guy carves your name in his egg foo young or hides the ring in a crème cheese wonton even if you crack a tooth finding it, and you think everyone else craves the same experience."

Adam grinned. "So what you're telling us is…no sky writing?"

Sally gave a disappointed groan, picked up the bottle of burgundy, and headed for the door. "Midwesterners," she muttered loud enough for them to hear. "Can't wait to see what your wedding will be like. A keg of beer, some sparklers, and three kinds of potato salad after the preacher man pronounces you man and wife down along the cow pasture."

"Don't worry, you aren't invited!" Billie called after her.

The sound of the front door banging shut was her reply.

She sighed. "Why can't people just be happy for other people instead of always trying to rewrite the occasion to fit *their* dreams?"

"Don't ask me," Adam said, watching her shut down the computer. "I'm a guy. I don't dream about getting married. Talk about nightmares!"

"If your music doesn't pan out, I'm sure you'll have a bright future in comedy. You should take your routine to the Standup Club downtown. They have a lot of drive-by shootings."

"Ouch! Is that how you share the love in your moment of joy? You should be ecstatic. Run off and call Mom and inform her you've finally said yes to a man, so she can start counting down the days until grandchildren begin popping out."

She ignored his teasing for the most part but her lips tightened at mention of their mother. When they exited the door of the winery Sally's car was already gone; a haze of gravel dust left in its wake.

"You did say yes, didn't you?"

She stuck her hand two inches from his nose. "Of course I said yes. How else would I get this ring?"

"True."

He kept pace with her as she strode toward the house. The temperature had dropped with the sun. It felt almost comfortable. He wasn't accustomed to ninety-degree weather at the end of September, but he supposed he could learn to live with it. Snow and ice would make a much better vacation get-away than dealing with it for nine months of the year.

Inside, Billie flipped lights on as she hurried through the house. She never could stand to be in an unlit room. He understood now the reason for that, and regretted teasing her about it when she was a teenager. The fancy leather couch greeted him when he stepped into the living room. He chose the recliner instead and stretched out with a sigh of contentment.

"You want something to drink?" Billie called from the kitchen.

"No thanks."

A couple minutes later she joined him, a cola in hand, and plopped down on the couch. She took a long drink and laid her head back, her legs stretched out and crossed at the ankles.

Adam watched her from beneath his lashes. She looked exhausted. Even with the glow of happiness about her, there was a hint of disappointment. She opened her eyes and caught him watching her.

"What are you looking at?"

He grinned, but refrained from using one of the timeless brotherly comebacks that quickly formed on his tongue. He noticed whenever she sat on the couch she always stroked the leather as though remembering something. "Mom said your furniture was ripped up when Sean Parker broke in that night. That must have been quite a shock."

She ran a finger down the seam of the armrest. "A visit from a mountain lion would have been preferable. Sean Parker's handiwork was from a violent and cruel mind."

"Sorry. I shouldn't have brought it up." His mother had told him of the man who raped Billie when she was a child; the reason she had suffered night terrors for years; the man who would soon be her father-in-law. At least he was safely behind prison bars for a good long time. Adam had never met him, but if the man showed up again while he was around, he'd make damn sure he never hurt another child.

For a moment he imagined a depth of unhealed pain flooded Billie's eyes, but then she shrugged. "It's all right. My therapist tells me that holding things in is not healthy. To think they go to school for eight long years to be able to spout that drivel." She grinned and changed the subject. "So, when are you going to figure out how to get Fredrickson Winery making money again instead of losing it? That's why I hired you, you know. Do you know a good magician?"

He pulled the lever of his chair and sat up straight to meet her at eye level. "No, but I have a better idea."

Her gaze widened in anticipation. "Do tell."

***

Margaret answered the phone on the third ring. Her hello was met with two seconds of dead air. Telemarketers again. She set the phone back in its cradle, then stood there staring at the thing. She didn't believe in premonitions, but felt sure it would ring again. Even though she'd anticipated it, when it rang the sound still made her jump. She tentatively reached out and picked it up.

"Hello? Margaret? Are you there?"

"Adam," she finally responded. His deep baritone was already familiar and strangely comforting. She relaxed and leaned against the kitchen counter. "What's up?"

"Are you busy? Cause I can call back later."

She smiled against the receiver. She definitely had this guy doing somersaults to please her. On the one hand, she was flattered. On the other hand, she didn't want to come across as controlling or a shrew. She could be spontaneous when she tried. Sometimes she even allowed Davy to stay up past his bedtime on a school night or gardened in the heat of the afternoon rather than the morning.

Davy was taking a shower before bed and Handel hadn't come home from the office yet. She was alone— for the moment. Not that she needed to be alone to speak with Adam on the telephone. After all, what would he have to say that would require privacy?

"Now's fine. What is it?"

"Just wondered if you could get away for a while. Take a walk with me. So we could talk."

"Talk?" She felt like a parrot repeating the word, but she couldn't think of anything else to say. His request scared her more than if he'd asked to sleep with her. She'd learned to handle those kinds of requests over the years, to have a quick comeback, to wilt a guy's advances with her "back off" glare. But this—talking while walking—backlit by the moon and stars, would require interaction—maybe even kissing...

She felt heat rise up her neck. Where the heck had that thought come from? She had no intention of kissing Adam Fredrickson. She heard the shower shut off in the bathroom down the hall. Davy would be in his pajamas and running out to say goodnight any minute. She couldn't leave him all alone in the house while she walked around outside with some man she'd barely met, talking and laughing and…definitely not kissing!

"Margaret? You still there?"

She clutched the receiver closer to her ear and glanced down the hall. "Yeah, I'm here. What did you want to talk about? Can't it wait until tomorrow night? You're still coming for dinner, aren't you?"

"Of course. I just thought since our siblings are taking the plunge that maybe we should get to know each other better. In fact, Billie sort of gave me the idea. She said walking through the vineyard at night was a good place to think and…"

"The plunge?"

"Yeah, you know…"

"No, I don't know. What are you talking about?" She had a sudden sinking feeling in the pit of her stomach. She sat down on one of the stools and rested her elbows on the counter, her head with the phone pressed to her ear cradled in her hands.

"Hasn't Handel told you…?"

She heard the garage door opening. "He's here now. I've got to go." She didn't wait for a response. She pressed the disconnect button and dropped the phone to the counter.

Handel pushed through the door with his suit coat draped over one arm and his briefcase in the other. He smiled cheerfully. "Hey, how's it going? Is Davy in bed yet? I have some news I'd like to share with both of you."

She shook her head. "He'll be out in a minute."

"Great." Handel set down his things and opened the refrigerator door. "What'd you have for dinner? I'm starved."

"There's spaghetti in that blue plastic container."

He pulled it out, popped the top off, and stuck it in the microwave to heat. "It's been quite a day," he said. With a silly grin plastered across his face, he leaned against the counter and faced her, his hands pushed in the front pockets of his slacks.

She heard the bathroom door bang open and a couple seconds later Davy charged into the kitchen, wet hair slickly combed over his forehead, his Spiderman pajamas clinging to his still damp body. "Uncle Handel! I got two goals today at practice!" he announced loud and proud.

Handel grinned, and high-fived his soggy nephew.

"Didn't you even dry off before you put those on?" she asked.

"I forgot to bring a towel in the bathroom, so I just rolled on the rug a little bit first. I'm pretty dry."

Handel laughed. "Next time I forget my towel, I'm gonna try that."

"Don't you dare!" she said, trying to hide a grin. "You are such a bad example to my son."

He shrugged. "Sorry. I do my best. I can't help it if he turned out goofy. It's probably from bouncing that ball off his head all the time."

"No, it's not!" Davy burst out. "My teacher said exercise is good." He got in his announcement pose, hands on hips, chin lifted slightly for emphasis. "She said that kids need to exercise everyday and eat vegetables and fruits cause there's aah…epi…demic of obisity in schools."

Margaret raised her brows. "You mean, obesity?"

"Yeah, that's what I said."

"Isn't his teacher about two hundred fifty pounds? Maybe she should start playing soccer," Handel whispered in Margaret's ear before turning to take his food out of the microwave.

"Did you brush your teeth, Davy?" she asked, to divert the conversation and because he had been known to skip that little procedure if he could get away with it.

"Why do you always ask the same question every night?"

"Why are you answering a question with a question? Did you or didn't you?"

He turned around and tromped back to the bathroom.

Handel chuckled as he sat at the table with his dinner. "He may turn out to be a great lawyer someday if we can break him of soccer before it knocks all the sense out of him." He took a bite of spaghetti.

"Just because you didn't play soccer in school doesn't mean he shouldn't. Everyone can't be on the nerdy debate team." She pulled out the chair across from him and sat down. He seemed so calm and collected, for a guy who had recently changed the course of his life by popping the question. Why hadn't he told her he was going to do that today?

"Hey, I take offense at that. I may have been nerdy then, but look at me now."

She shook her head. "Only in court do you reign supreme. Outside in the real world, you're still the same older brother I remember with a bad haircut and pimples."

"I haven't had my hair cut in ages and my pimples are pretty much forgotten, so what are you so ticked about?" he asked perceptively, his gaze locked with hers.

She tried to shrug it off, but she couldn't. The way it made her feel when Adam called and told her about Handel and Billie was too personal, too close to the surface. Her eyes filled with tears and she looked away. "I just thought after all we've been through that you would tell me before you made important decisions— life changing decisions for all of us."

"What are you…" His lips spread into a thin line and he put down his fork. He reached out and covered her hand with his. "I'm sorry. I should have talked with you about it first. I didn't think. It was sort of spur of the moment, emotions running high kind of a thing. I wanted to be the first to tell you. I didn't think you'd find out before I got home."

"Adam called," she said, and wiped at her eyes. "He assumed I already knew."

"Oh, terrific. Billie's brother has managed to tick you off again. I guess I can forget the happy blended family wedding, huh?"

She managed a smile and shook her head. "No, he didn't tick me off. Actually, you're the one I'm mad at, but I'll try to forgive you since you're my brother and all."

"Forgive him for what?" Davy asked, suddenly at her elbow, a dab of toothpaste still clinging to his upper lip.

She wiped it away with the pad of her thumb. "For not sharing his surprise sooner."

"You have a surprise? What is it?"

Handel pushed his plate to the side and donned his serious face. "I asked Billie to marry me today and I was hoping that the two of you would give me away."

"Give you away?" Davy scrunched his eyes up in a frown. "What does that mean?"

Margaret rolled her eyes. "We would be glad to give you away. Where do we sign up?"

Handel stood up and came around the table to take them both into his arms for a group hug. "You two are my family and always will be. Billie is just joining the tribe. It won't change the way I feel about you or what you can expect of me. I will always be here for you when you need me. That's a promise."

Margaret hugged him back, knowing that things always change and there was really nothing she could do about it but go with the flow or swim against the current. She couldn't ruin Handel's chance at happiness, so she would float along and hope there weren't any jagged rocks hiding just below the surface.

CHAPTER SIX

Margaret walked up and down the few rows of Parker vines, carefully inspecting the heavy clusters of purple and partially green orbs. They were nearly ready. The smell of ripening fruit was heady, almost overpowering. She plucked a grape and popped it in her mouth, relishing the burst of sweet, tart flavor. A few more days.

Every winemaker knew that ninety-five percent of good winemaking began with the perfect grapes. She had them. The other five percent from the winemaker's personal touch and style. This year's crop would prove her ability and technique. She just had to follow through.

She heard the approach of a vehicle and turned, her hand up to shield her eyes from the bright afternoon sun. A sleek blue convertible sports car pulled up to the house. A man wearing a white collared shirt opened the car door and stepped out. The way he moved was familiar. He stood looking up at the house a moment before turning toward the vineyard, and pulling off his sunglasses. Even at this distance she recognized him.

August.

No. She wouldn't think of him as she once did. The nickname had been an endearment. Agosto Salvatore was nothing to her now. The man who left her pregnant and brokenhearted at fifteen, who fled to Italy without a thought for anyone but himself, did not deserve respect, let alone a pet name. For ten long years he hadn't tried to get in touch with her or have any contact with his son. He may have grown older, but she doubted he had grown kinder. Why had he returned now, after all these years?

He lifted a hand in greeting, hooked his glasses in the front of his shirt, and ambled slowly across the yard toward the vineyard as though she'd been expecting him. He was the last person she'd expected or wanted to see, and yet she knew he'd return, despite desperate prayers to the contrary.

She suddenly wondered what she must look like in worn out jeans with holes in the knees and one of Handel's castoff t-shirts splattered with blue and green paint. She supposed it was human nature to want him to desire her and regret his choice ten years ago, even though the last thing she wanted was a face-to-face confrontation with the man.

"Ciao, Margaret," he said, a slow smile climbing his face till his dark eyes glinted with that sexy light that once made her weak in the knees. He ran his fingers through his hair, brushing it smoothly from his forehead. It was still thick and wavy and for a moment she couldn't help remembering the feel of it in her hands when they kissed.

She licked her lips and tried to appear unimpressed with his fit, tanned body and playboy good looks. "What are you doing here? I told you not to come back."

"I didn't think you truly meant it. That man who was here before…does he work here?" he asked, glancing nervously back toward the house.

"What do you want, Agosto?" she asked, ignoring the question. Let him worry. Adam was younger, more muscular, and a head taller. She doubted Agosto would want to have a run-in with him. Perhaps it would keep him from overstaying his visit.

"You know what I want. I already told your brother. I want to spend time with my son. He needs to know his father. Where he comes from. Who he is."

"My son knows exactly who he is. He doesn't need you to tell him that, or to buy him fancy toys to convolute the message. He's smart and kind and honest and generous. He's a Parker, through and through. You had your chance to know him and now it's too late." She gripped the picking shears she held and tried to calm her temper.

His gaze turned steely and she knew from experience that he expected to get his way, no matter what it took. "I don't want to bring the court system into our private affairs, but if you give me no other choice…"

"How dare you come here with your rich man attitude and think you can take what you want. This is America, not Italy. And here you're just a deadbeat dad who deserted his son and hasn't paid a cent to help raise him. So, get in your fancy car and go home." She turned and started walking away. Fear tightened screws down on her heart. The thought of losing Davy through some fluke of the court system made her physically ill. She had to get away from him before he saw how frightened his words made her feel.

"Please." The word vibrated with emotion. She'd never heard him beg before.

She stopped and stood still.

"I'm sorry for running away. I was just a boy and didn't realize how much I would regret it. Leaving you. Leaving my son." He paused, and cleared his throat. "Please…won't you give me a chance?"

She slowly turned and met his eyes, pleading and needy. She'd never seen this side of him. He looked down at the ground for a second as though trying to pull himself together and then stepped forward and tentatively held out a hand.

"Can you try to forgive me? Maybe not for your sake, but for our son's. I understand that he doesn't need me. But I need him."

She wanted to believe him, *needed* to believe. She reached out and took his hand and then just as quickly released it. The contact was too much, too soon. "I'll try," she said, her voice husky. "But I need to speak with Handel before I make any decisions."

Agosto's lips tightened at mention of her brother, but he nodded. "Thank you, Margaret." He pulled a business card from his wallet and handed it to her. "My cell number. Will you call me when you have made a decision?"

She nodded, took the card and stuck it in her back pocket without looking at it.

He slipped his sunglasses on and smiled. "I look forward to meeting my son," he said, as though it were a done deal.

Margaret stood rooted to the spot, until his car disappeared back down the driveway and sped away into the hot afternoon. Then she ran into the house and called Handel.

***

Adam followed Mario around the vineyard and winery all day, asking questions and mostly getting grunts and nods. Mario's English was worse than his Spanish, so it was a real learning experience. The man tended Billie's vines as if each cluster of grapes was already worth a hundred dollars a bottle. He certainly hoped they were.

"Sneep," Mario said. The man pointed at the cluster of plump grapes and made a scissor motion with his right hand.

Adam used the cutting tool he'd been handed and snipped the cluster from the vine. He held it in the palm of his hand like a newborn. Mario plucked a grape from the cluster and bit it in half. He chewed thoughtfully and said something in Spanish. Then held out the other half for Adam to inspect.

"Nice grape," Adam said, unsure what was expected of him.

Mario grunted and shook his head. He turned and headed back to the red pickup parked at the end of the field, his short legs, encased in baggy khakis, made quick time over the rough dirt track. Adam assumed the lesson was over and followed. He popped a grape in his mouth and chewed slowly, trying to get an idea of what Mario was so excited about. Not that he was a connoisseur of grunts, but it seemed that his grunts had escalated as they'd checked grapes on each acre and nearly every row.

He glanced toward the Parker place. A blue convertible was backing away from the house. He was too far away to see the driver, but from the make and model of the vehicle, they must be loaded. He'd never be rich enough to drive a car like that. Probably some wealthy dude from San Francisco out touring wineries and got lost. The car turned onto the highway and was soon out of sight. He glanced back at the house and saw Margaret sprinting in from the field. A moment later she yanked open the garage access door and disappeared inside.

Mario tapped the horn of the pickup. Adam hurried to catch up. He opened the passenger door and climbed in. They rode the rutted road back around to the winery and Mario parked in the shade of a big tree. He took the box with the sample clusters they'd collected from each row and hurried across the gravel parking area, his work boots kicking up a cloud of dust with each step. Adam followed and pulled open the winery door for the man.

"Hey you two. Been out in the fields all this time?" Sally said when they stopped at the front office. "You look a little sunburned, Minnesota," she teased.

"Miss Fredrickson?" Mario interrupted, intent on his purpose.

Sally hooked a thumb toward the back of the building. "She's in the barrel room, I think."

Mario started down the hallway.

"You better pick up a bottle of water in the fridge first. You looked parched."

Adam wiped his forehead with the sleeve of his t-shirt. "It must be ninety degrees today. Glad I'm not wearing a hooded sweatshirt like Mario. That man soaks up heat like a rock. It doesn't faze him."

"He's used to it. You, on the other hand, look just this side of a heatstroke."

"I'll survive. Besides, the barrel room is in the cellar, right? It's cool down there." He turned to follow Mario and stopped. He poked his head back in the door. "Sally, do you know anyone that drives a blue convertible Ferrari?"

Her brows went up along with her interest. "No, but I'm open to an introduction. Love me a powerful engine." She stood up and moved toward the window. "Someone visiting the winery?"

He shook his head. "Just saw one over at the Parker place."

"Probably one of Handel's rich clients."

"He has a lot of wealthy clients?"

She shrugged. "I don't know. I've heard rumors. Some say he's in bed with mobsters, but I think it's just jealous talk. He's beaten some of the best attorneys around, and they all hate to lose. Winning is inbred in them, or at the very least, force-fed to them in law school."

His gaze narrowed. "You can't really believe that—about the mobsters. My sister would never get involved with someone like that."

Sally laughed and shook her head, moving back to her desk. "I said there were rumors. I didn't say I believed them. I've known Handel nearly his entire life. He's a good guy."

Sometimes he had a hard time knowing when Sally was joking and when she was serious. He released the breath of a laugh. "Just call me gullible."

"I do," she said with a grin, "daily."

He went in search of the barrel room. A flight of stairs led down to the lower level where the temperature instantly dropped another fifteen degrees. The change in temperature cooled the sweat in his shirt and sent a chill down his arms.

"There you are." Billie waved him over.

Billie, Mario, and Ernesto inspected and tasted the grapes. Mario spoke in rapid Spanish and Ernesto interpreted for Billie's sake. She nodded, clearly excited. Adam looked around the big room. Large barrels were stacked in special racks, lying on their sides three deep, filling the long cellar.

Billie thanked Mario, who grunted something in return and followed the other man back up the stairs. Adam didn't know if he was supposed to keep tagging along, but he preferred the cool cellar, so he stayed behind.

"Mario thinks we need to start harvesting by the end of the week. Timing is everything. Are you ready to experience Crush in the Napa Valley?" Billie asked, her voice sounding a tad stressed.

He ran his hand along one of the smooth Oak barrels. "I don't know if I'm ready, but I'll do my best to be a help and not a hindrance. Are you ready?"

She bit at her bottom lip and nodded. "I think so. Don't have much of a choice. Ready or not, the grapes ripen for picking, and the wine needs to be made." She slowly inhaled and released a breath. "I've decided to close the tasting room during harvest. All the other wineries will be closed anyway, so traffic will be sparse. We'll just have to get by without that extra income."

Upstairs again, they stopped in Billie's office and she rifled through some paperwork on her desk. "I need to have Sally call and make sure the new barrels will be here on time. We're going to try something new this year. A white table wine."

"Have you spoken with Margaret yet?"

"Not yet. I thought maybe you'd sound her out for me. You are having dinner with her tonight, right?" She glanced up from the papers and smiled. "I'm not sure what to think about that. I thought she disliked you at first sight, but now you're—what? Dating?"

He slouched in one of the chairs facing her desk, his hands laced behind his head. "I wouldn't call it dating, but she definitely digs me."

"Reeeallly." She stretched the word out in her most sarcastic tone.

He nodded. "Yes. Really. At least she likes me better than that slimy rich Italian that dropped by in his biggo limo."

Her eyes widened. "What Italian?"

"Some guy she really despises. You think she took an instant dislike to me, you should have seen the look on her face when we pulled up and he was there. She didn't even want to talk to him. She ordered him off her property and told him never to come back. I suppose he's some creep she dated or something. She didn't say."

Billie set the papers back on the desk and opened her mouth to speak, then apparently thought better of it. She cleared her throat and picked up her cell phone to check for messages.

"What?"

She shook her head. "If she wanted you to know, she would have told you."

"You've got to be kidding me." He leaned forward in the chair. "You know something I should know and you're not going to tell me? If I wait for her to open up, I'll be a century old."

"He's the one," she said, leaning against the edge of the desk.

"The one?"

"The man who broke Margaret's heart and changed her forever."

He frowned. "That's giving a lot of power to this guy. Margaret didn't seem that taken with him." He did remember the fear in her eyes and the way she had to psych herself up before getting out of the car and confronting him though.

Billie nibbled at her lip for a second. "He's also Davy's father."

The bottom suddenly dropped out of the ride he was on.

***

Handel leaned across the table, driving his point home with expressive hand movements as though he were in court. "You can't trust him. You know that. Even Carl said his cousin is scum. And you know Carl is proud of his family tree. He still blames himself for allowing Agosto within a hundred feet of you ten years ago."

Margaret got up from the kitchen chair and paced to the refrigerator and back, unable to sit still or hold her brother's piercing gaze. She couldn't think straight. Ever since Agosto had used that word—a word she'd never heard from him before—something cracked. Maybe it was the ice dam that had been jamming up her feelings, only allowing anger and resentment to escape for the longest time. She didn't know. She did know that one word did not negate ten years of silence, but still…

"Margaret. Don't give in to him. We can hold him up in court for years. He'll get bored and fly home soon enough. He's always taken the easy route in everything. If it requires time and patience, he'll disappear. Why put Davy through that unnecessarily?"

She stopped pacing and slumped back into the chair, propping her head in her hands. Davy had her. He had Handel. Was that enough? She used to think it was, but now she wasn't so sure. Was she withholding his chance to know his father for all the wrong reasons? He already thought she hated men. Maybe that wasn't far from the truth. Maybe letting go of long-held bitterness and resentment would allow Davy an opportunity he deserved.

She sat up and smoothed a loose strand of hair behind her ear. "I don't know anymore, Handel. I've been holding on to this anger for so long and today he didn't seem like the monster I framed him to be. He seemed different, mature, ready to take responsibility. Maybe he's right. Davy should know…"

"No! He's wrong." Handel cut in, his voice taking on that commanding tone that made her rebel ten years ago and still had the ability to make her feel like *little sister in need of a talking to.* "He's just manipulating you. There is definitely a reason he wants to meet Davy, but I doubt it has anything to do with love or responsibility."

"You don't know that. People can change. And it doesn't really matter what you think because he's my son and I'll make the decision," she snapped.

She saw the hurt in his eyes but it was too late to take it back. He scooted his chair away from the table and stood up. "I'll be home late," he said, his voice soft now. "I have to interview a client and finish up a case." He went to the door, picked up his briefcase, and looked back. "Please don't make any decisions you'll regret. I can't bear to see you hurt again like before."

When the door closed behind him, Margaret swiped at a tear that slipped down her cheek. She went to the front window and watched him drive away. His face was set in that stony way she remembered the day he learned she was pregnant with Agosto's child. She thought he was angry with her, disappointed and disgusted, but she soon realized that it wasn't her he was angry with. He'd gone after Agosto later that day at Carl's restaurant. If not for Carl stepping in, her brother would probably be in jail for beating the father of her child to death. Carl drove Agosto directly to the airport after that confrontation and made sure he flew back to Italy a day ahead of the ticket he'd already purchased.

She didn't want to hurt Handel. He'd taken care of her, made sure she and Davy had everything they needed. He was her family and she trusted him. But what if he was wrong? What is Davy needed to know his father? What if someday her son resented her for keeping him in the dark? Could she live with that?

She pulled Agosto's business card out of her jeans pocket and read the words printed in burgundy-colored font. *Salvatore Imports & Exports*. A fancy gold embossed logo with the Salvatore crest resided in the upper left corner. She stared at it for a moment and wondered what her life would have been like if he'd really loved her, if everything he told her wasn't a big fat lie.

What ifs? What a crock! She threw the card in the junk drawer with the telephone book no one ever used anymore and slammed it shut. Apparently, residual anger was still slipping through the cracks of her ice dam and slowing the flow of forgiveness, because the past was still pretty fresh in her mind.

***

"Has Agosto been by here?" Handel asked, watching Carl chop Portabella mushrooms with quick and accurate precision. He scraped them into a heated skillet and let one of his assistants take over.

Without looking up, Carl yelled something to the Sous-chef in Italian and wiped his hands on a towel. He headed toward the back door and Handel followed him out into the alley. A busboy sat smoking on the closed lid of the garbage bin. Carl jabbed his chin toward the door and the boy crushed out his cigarette and slunk back inside.

"What do you want from me?" Carl spread his hands and lifted his shoulders in a helpless gesture. He looked tired. His face was already dark with a five-o'clock shadow although he probably didn't come in until noon. He was up late every night and lived on a different clock than most of the business world. The restaurant opened at four p.m. and didn't close until midnight. "I don't like what he did to your sister anymore than you, but he is Davy's father and he says he wants to do right by him."

Handel raised his brows. "Right by him? You've got to be kidding. Nine years after the fact of his birth he wants to do right by him? Now? Why?" He threw his hands up in frustration. "You know better than I that Agosto doesn't do anything out of the goodness of his heart. I want to know what he's up to."

Carl shook his head. "I don't know. He came here and apologized for the past. Offered his hand of friendship." He met Handel's steely gaze. "What was I supposed to do? He's family."

"And what are we—chump change?" Handel moved past him toward the door but Carl stopped him with a hand on his arm.

"Just because I accepted his apology doesn't mean I trust him. I already made a call to my mother. If anyone can find out what he's up to, she can."

Handel turned and clasped his friend's hand. "Thank you. I'm sorry to come here like this during business hours. I've just been so worried about

Margaret. Davy means everything to her. You know that."

"I know." Carl nodded. "By the way, I hear congratulations are in order."

"News travels way too fast. I wanted to tell you myself." He grinned. "Since you're the closest thing I have to a brother and I know you already own a tux, I was hoping you'd agree to be my best man."

Carl laughed and threw his arms around Handel. "I'd be honored." He pulled away and straightened his white chef coat. "Now I've got to get back in there and make sure Andre hasn't ruined my pesto sauce." He yanked open the door and let Handel go in first. "Tell Billie I expect you two to be in soon to celebrate. On me."

CHAPTER SEVEN

The smell of grilling meat made Adam head around the corner of the house instead of knocking at the door. Smoke signals wafted over to meet his nose and he felt his stomach rumble. It had been a while since he'd had a decent steak. He was too broke for such extravagance in college and his mother rarely cooked red meat anymore. She had decided it was unhealthy because she heard some talk show host spouting the horrors of mad cow disease or something. Well, he'd rather go mad from beef than live on tuna fish and salad for the rest of his life.

Margaret had her back to him, standing over the grill with a long fork in hand, flipping meat and rearranging foil wrapped potatoes. She hummed an old rock melody in an off-key sort of way that made him smile. In short shorts, her legs appeared to stretch a long, tan mile. She turned around and nearly jabbed him with the fork when she saw him standing there.

"You scared me!" she accused. She glanced at her watch. "Aren't you a bit early? I haven't even changed yet."

He gave her an appraising look. "Don't change for my benefit. I think you look terrific already." He took the fork out of her hand, as she was still pointing it menacingly toward him and approached the grill. "Need any help? Smells great."

She pulled open the sliding door and stepped through. "You want something cold to drink?"

"Sure. Whatever you're having."

Her lips turned up slightly. "All right." She slid the door closed and disappeared.

Adam sat down in one of the green mesh patio chairs and stretched his legs out. It had been a long day following Mario around the winery, learning all he could in a blitz-sized lesson plan in a Spanish immersion class. He looked out across Margaret's vineyard to Fredrickson's and beyond. The valley was awash with a mellow pink and orange glow. The setting sun reflected off shiny, dark, grape leaves fluttering in the breeze, as shadows stretched long from trees and poles.

He laid the fork on the table and crossed his arms over his chest. He didn't know how to safely bring up the subject of Agosto Salvatore, but he couldn't get it off his mind. She would probably accuse him of sticking his nose in her private business, which was what he would be doing. But he couldn't be neutral when it came to Margaret Parker.

"Here you go." She stepped through the slider, a frosted glass in each hand.

He jumped up and took the drink she offered. "Thanks."

She checked on the food and closed the grill lid. "Almost done. You do like your steaks pink inside, don't you? Cause I prefer not to ruin a perfectly good t-bone by incinerating it."

He grinned and raised his glass in salute. "My kind of woman."

"You're not just saying that to get on my good side, are you?"

"Which side would that be? They both look good to me."

She shook her head and sighed. "How long have you been practicing this routine?"

"As a Fredrickson it just comes natural. You noticed how quickly my sister got her hooks into Handel."

"With those two I think it was mutual." She turned away to open the grill and placed the steaks and potatoes on a platter.

With her back to him, Adam found it easier to ask a hard question. "Why are you upset about their engagement then? Shouldn't true love be worthy of celebration?"

She shut off the gas and closed the lid before turning slowly around with the platter in hand. "I thought we'd eat inside since it's getting dark," she said, her voice hard and flat.

He pulled the slider open and watched her go inside ahead of him. She moved stiffly erect as though an angry puppet master had a hold of her heartstrings. He followed slowly, carrying their drinks, wondering how he managed to stick a size twelve foot into his mouth so easily.

The dining room table was set with white china edged with swirls of black and red. Two candles served as a centerpiece, already lit and flickering in the low light of the room. A bottle of wine and two long-stemmed glasses completed the picture. She'd done all this for him and he'd just screwed it up.

She set the platter down on the corner of the table and motioned for him to sit. "Let's eat before it gets cold."

As he took his place at the table, she flipped the lights on and leaned over to blow out the candles before taking her chair. A thin wisp of smoke wafted toward him and he waved it away. "I'm sorry. I thought you were upset about their engagement. When I talked to you on the phone you sounded angry."

She laid her fork down and met his eyes. "I wasn't angry. I was surprised. You managed to turn what should have been a happy announcement into a sad *why am I the last one to know* moment. You seem to have the ability to change the simplest occasions into dramatic events. Why do you do that? Hmm?"

"I didn't know I did." He leaned forward and picked up the bottle of wine. "May I?" He filled both goblets and sat back, lifting his slightly toward her, a tentative gesture of apology. "To new friends, future family, and the ability to reconcile them both."

She lifted her wine glass and clinked them gently together. The ting of Crystal reverberated softly and then they drank, eyes locked over cold candles. She watched him expectantly. Was he missing something? He licked his lips and took another sip.

"Wow, this is really great wine. Is it from Fredrickson's?"

"No." She smiled, clearly pleased that he liked it. "It's mine."

"Yours? What do you mean?"

"Did you think your sister is the only woman who knows how to make wine? I've been bottling my own for a few years now. I just sell it locally by word of mouth. Handel's friend, Carl, buys most of it for his restaurant. Handel calls it my hobby, but it's really my passion. I love to experiment, try new things. This year's crop looks amazing. I'm pretty sure it will be the best batch ever." She served a steak and potato on each of their plates. Offered him butter and sour cream.

"I hope Fredrickson's can say the same. Mario seemed pleased when we sampled the grapes today."

"He should be. They look good."

"Been checking out the competition?" he asked. He cut into his steak and took a bite, savoring the smoky, beef flavor. It was perfectly pink inside and nicely blackened on the outside. Excellent.

"Fredrickson's has never been competition. I grew up here. I don't know if you heard, but my grandfather once owned the winery. Handel and I still feel part of it. Our DNA is in that soil, sprouts up in those vines each year, and is now bottled under the Fredrickson label."

"Very evocative picture you paint there."

"Perhaps. It's the way I feel." She took a bite of steak and chewed thoughtfully. "I always felt that someday the winery would be ours again, because it's in our blood. But Handel really doesn't have a desire to get into the business. He's good at what he does. Law. I, on the other hand, have always longed for what I couldn't have."

"So, if you were given the chance to oversee the winemaking over there and help turn things around, would you jump at it, or are you waiting for my sister to go bankrupt so you can pick it up for a pittance and get it back under the Parker name?"

She took a sip of wine and watched him over the rim of her glass. "None of this land will ever go for a pittance. As small as Fredrickson's is, it's worth millions." She laughed at his shocked expression. "You didn't know your sister was considered a millionaire?"

"I never really thought about it that way."

"Probably wise. Easy come, easy go. So tell me," she said, assuming a bland expression, "how do you make a small fortune in the wine business?"

He shrugged. "I don't know."

"You start with a large fortune and buy a winery." She picked up the bottle and refilled their glasses. "Sorry. That's a lame joke every vintner in the valley has probably heard and repeated a thousand times. But sadly, it's true. This business is not just about money. It has to be in your blood. You have to love everything about it, or you might as well sell out and go home."

"Does that mean you'll take the job working for Billie, or are you waiting for her to go home?"

Her eyes widened and she set her glass down with a slight thunk, sloshing wine over the rim. "You're serious?" she said, wiping it up with a napkin.

"As serious as a monk in a monastery."

"She really wants me? She thinks I can do the job?"

"You'll have to convince her of that. But she's willing to give you a try. She told me to ask you to come by tomorrow about ten and set things in motion."

A smile spread across her face, but her eyes glistened with tears on the verge of overflowing. She got up and started clearing dishes, as though to distract herself from feeling.

"Are you all right?" he asked, handing her the empty platter and his iced tea glass, hoping she'd realize he was still working on his steak and not ready to relinquish it into her hands. He cut another bite and jammed it in his mouth, already full of potato.

She suddenly stopped mid-motion and started laughing. She set the dishes down on the counter and came back to the table. "I'm so sorry. I didn't give you a chance to finish." She pulled her bottom lip between her teeth like an embarrassed young girl. "You must think I'm crazy."

He shook his head, his mouth still full.

She sat down across from him and lifted her glass once again. Her eyes sparkled with happiness and tears—apparently, one and the same with her. "Thank you, Adam. You don't know how much this means to me."

He swallowed and lifted his glass. "Actually, I think I do. Having the opportunity to live your dream is more than most of us ever realize. I wish you the very best year of winemaking and a successful partnership with Fredrickson's."

They finished the bottle and Adam suggested he get his guitar from the backseat of the car and play her something. The front porch light came on as he descended the steps and he thought he saw someone move into the shadow of the trees along the drive. He stopped and stared into the dark. "Hello?" he called out. The breeze played lightly over vegetation, rustling leaves and rippling grass. He supposed it could have been a dog or maybe just his imagination.

He grabbed his guitar and ran back up the steps and into the house. Margaret was whistling somewhere past the kitchen. He followed the sound and found her in a back room that looked like a family hangout. A comfy couch, chairs, and a piano filled the small space, along with a bookcase stuffed to capacity. Books lay in piles on the floor and on a small coffee table as well. A fireplace jutted out from one wall in black and grey brick, the hearth a good three feet deep.

Margaret sat curled in the corner of the old couch, her feet drawn up under her and a magazine in her hands. She turned the pages as though looking for a specific article. She glanced up. "Have a seat. I was trying to find something I read a while back. A company makes oak spirals that can be pushed right into the tanks. You get the oak flavor and aging without the expense of oak barrels. I think that would cut our budget by quite a lot."

"Wow, you really meant it when you said winemaking was your passion," he said, leaning his guitar against the wall.

"Here it is!" she said, as though he hadn't even spoken. "I'll show this to Billie in the morning." She bent the page over and set the magazine on the overloaded coffee table. Then she met his amused gaze. "I didn't want to forget."

"Of course not."

She glanced toward his guitar. "Aren't you going to play me one of your songs?"

"Maybe later. I thought we could talk and get to know one another better." He sat down at the other end of the sofa and hooked a leg up on the cushion to face her.

She turned slightly toward him, her arm slung across the back of the couch. "Sounds like you have an agenda."

"Not an agenda. Interested in you, that's all."

"How old are you?" she asked.

"What does that have to do with anything?"

"It has something to do with everything. If you were an older man, people might say you were taking advantage of me. But since I'm older, they'd probably call me a cougar or some other cat name."

She said it with a smile and yet he could tell she was closer to serious than not. She rested her head on her hand and watched him for a reaction. He wouldn't give her what she wanted. "I don't think anyone would consider a two year age difference to be cougaristic. It's not as if I'm a teenager in your Sunday school class."

"I don't think that's a word."

"Cougaristic? It's most certainly a word. I just coined it."

"Well, cougaristic or not, you're too young for me. So get it out of your head that we are dating. We're not." She held his gaze unwaveringly as though to look away would lose the argument.

"I didn't say anything about us dating," he said, inwardly pleased when she shifted her gaze to the coffee table. A tell tale sign that it wasn't the answer she expected—or perhaps desired. "Not that there would be anything wrong with it. But I think we have a few things to get out of the way first."

"What are you talking about? I said we weren't dating and that's that."

"I need to know how you feel about this Italian dude. He's much more to you than you let on."

She lifted her head and her mouth opened but nothing came out for a second. He could see she was mentally sifting through the information. He'd blind-sided her. "Who have you been talking to?" she demanded.

"I saw him here again today in his fancy car. I was worried about you so I asked Billie about him." He didn't want to bring his sister into it, but he'd never been good at lying. "She told me he's Davy's father."

Margaret jumped up from the couch and glared down at him. "How dare you? You blow into town and start tearing into my life like you have a right. You don't. I don't care if you are Billie's brother. My personal life is not open to scrutiny."

He stood up and faced her, wanting to reach out and pull her close, but restrained himself. "This has nothing to do with Billie. This is totally about us. You and me." He took a step closer. "I enjoy spending time with you and I'm attracted to you. I think if you admit it to yourself—you're attracted to me too. This two-year age difference is not a breaking point. It's not as if I'm an inexperienced frat boy trying to bed an older woman. You're twenty-five—not forty-five."

She licked her lips, her gaze riveted to his mouth. She moved in close and placed her hands flat against his chest. Close enough to kiss, but a breath shy of actual contact. "Is this what you want?" she asked softly. "Passion, excitement, the thrill of seduction?"

He pulled back and gently pushed her hands away. He knew a test when he felt one. "Of course it's what I want," he said, his voice thick with need. "What red-blooded man wouldn't want you? That's not what I came for though." He wanted to be absolutely truthful. She needed to know where he stood. "You've made your point. I am inexperienced. In relationships, in love, in life." He shook his head. "But not anymore than you are. Okay, you had sex with that guy and conceived a son, but were you in love with him, or was it just teenage hormones raging out of control? I've had that too. It wasn't anything to write a memoir about."

She turned away and moved out of reach. Sitting on the edge of the piano bench, she crossed her legs and released a quiet sigh. For just a moment he thought maybe she was giving him the silent treatment, but then she started talking. "Agosto was twenty when I met him. I was fifteen, going through a hell-bent rebellious stage. My parents were no longer around and Handel was my keeper. He tried to do right by me, to make sure I went to school and brushed my teeth and stayed away from bad influences, but he was busy with law school and had no idea what went through a teenage girl's mind." She made a self-deprecating sound and looked down at her hands twisting in her lap. "I just wanted to escape my life. Agosto seemed like the perfect channel."

"Did you love him?"

She looked up. "I thought I did. I was fifteen. Remember? But it didn't matter, because to him I was just a fling, a diversion to keep him from being bored while he was here. When I told him I was pregnant, he accused me of …" she closed her eyes and breathed deeply. "Doesn't matter anymore. The short version—I was an American tramp he could never take home to daddy. So he left without acknowledging his son and now he's returned—supposedly a more mature, responsible version of himself—and wants to get to know Davy." She fell silent, staring across the room at the cold fireplace.

Adam didn't know what to say. The raw pain still evident in her voice, said it all. He picked up his guitar and scooted to the edge of the couch. His fingers moved over the strings, holding, strumming, plucking a bluesy tune from memory. He closed his eyes and played, feeling the music vibrate through his fingers and fill his chest with the familiar ache of sadness and loss. He moved on to something a little jazzier and then riffed into a rendition of Heart's *Crazy on You*. The music tore through his fingers like a surge of electricity and up his arms. He stopped abruptly, his hand muting the strings vibration.

When he looked up she was staring at him like he had two heads and one of them had grown horns. "Wow," she drawled. "Wish I had a cigarette lighter, but this will have to do." She stood up, flipped open her cell phone and held it up, swaying to a silent beat.

Feeling embarrassed, he shook his head and set his guitar against the books piled on the table. "Thanks. A standing ovation from an audience of one. That's probably a first."

She smiled and snapped the phone closed, laid it on the piano. "Not possible. I'm sure you've had many standing ovations of one. Hasn't your mother listened to you play?"

"She thinks I'm wasting my time. Maybe she's right." He stood up and moved to the piano. She stepped back and watched him play chopsticks with robotic flair. He finished and turned to face her. "Music is a pipedream. Number crunching is a solid career. "

She moved in so fast he didn't have time to anticipate. Her fingers sank into his hair and pulled him close. Her lips were soft and supple and searching and he kissed her back with all the urgency she gave. She smelled of shampoo and tasted of wine, and he couldn't get enough of her.

The sound of the garage door opening outside was like a gunshot in a prison ward. She went stiff in his arms and pulled away, smoothing her hair and straightening her top. He moved off to stand at the bookcase and peruse the large collection of books and magazines. He didn't know if he looked innocent when Handel appeared in the doorway moments later, but he felt less than honest.

"Hey you two. What's up? Did I miss all the fun?" Handel ran a hand through his hair, pushing it back from his forehead. "I hope you left me some food. I'm starved."

Adam cleared his throat. "I s'pose I should be going." He turned and caught Margaret's eye. Her cheeks were pinker than they'd been a few minutes earlier.

"I'll walk you to the car," she said, her voice slightly breathless. Slipping past her brother, she said over her shoulder, "There's leftovers in the fridge, Handel. It's all yours."

Outside, Margaret nervously picked at a thumbnail, until Adam put his finger under her chin and lifted her gaze. "You really haven't dated since you were fifteen, have you?" he asked, knowing the answer.

"I've dated," she said, looking away over his shoulder.

"Really? Who?"

"I'm not the kind of girl who kisses and tells." She met his eyes.

He pushed a stray strand of hair away from her face and let his thumb gently caress her cheek. "Is that an invitation," he asked, even as he moved to capture her lips.

She kissed him back and finally pulled away, breathless. "Don't do that again," she warned, her voice filled with laughter.

"Why not?"

"I can't breathe."

He chuckled and pulled her close, loving the feel of her in his arms, her hair brushing his face. They slowly pulled apart and he opened the car door and climbed inside.

"Goodnight, music man."

"Night, Meg."

Out on the highway, he remembered that he left his guitar behind. And smiled at the thought of a sweet reunion concert.

CHAPTER EIGHT

Agosto paced in his hotel suite, intermittently stopping to stare out the window. Sailboats skimmed the blue waters of the bay and the Golden Gate Bridge stretched in the distance. But he couldn't really enjoy it. His plans were not coming together as quickly as he'd hoped and loose ends always made him nervous.

He knew Handel would be a problem. The man hated him. That's why finding an opportunity to speak with Margaret alone had been his first move. And he'd done a fabulous job of showing his vulnerable side. He stopped at the mirror and adjusted the collar of his shirt, brushed a speck of lint from his trousers. He smiled at his reflection. She was still not immune to his charm.

At first, she appeared impenetrable, hardened from past experience. But he knew American women and what made them tick. He'd said, *please*, and her reserve crumbled like damaged, pocked concrete. He could see it in her eyes, those blue depths that always gave away her feelings no matter how hard she tried to hide them.

He glanced at his watch. It had been two days. Why hadn't she called? Had Handel convinced her otherwise? His sources had informed him that Handel Parker was a formidable attorney in the courtroom, that he could probably convince a jury that Charles Manson was innocent if he tried. But he was Margaret's brother, not her attorney, and from what he remembered, she didn't like to be told what to do—especially by men.

His only option was to return to the Napa Valley and see this through personally. If she wouldn't initiate a meeting between him and his son, then he would just have to manage one himself. He picked up the phone and dialed the hotel desk.

"This is Agosto Salvatore. Please have my car brought round and have someone come and collect my bag in ten minutes."

He opened the closet and found his suitcase, threw it on the rumpled bed and began filling it with clothes from the armoire. He heard the water shut off in the shower and a minute later the door opened, releasing a cloud of steam and a tall, thin woman wearing one of the hotel's plush oversized robes. Strands of damp hair framed a face worthy of the ten-o'clock news. "Agosto," she said, her smooth brow wrinkling unattractively, "what are you doing?"

"Checking out." He turned to survey the closet, chose two pair of shoes and a suit, zipped them into a suit bag. He looked up and she was still staring at him as though he'd lost his mind.

"You said we were going to the track and then tonight you'd take me out for dinner," she said, tugging the belt of the robe tighter. "What's going on?"

"Get dressed and go home. I don't need you anymore." He snapped the suitcase latches closed and moved around her to get his things from the bathroom vanity.

She grabbed his arm. "Why are you doing this? I thought we had something…" her voice trailed off as she met his eyes, hard with impatience.

"We did. Now it's over." He pulled away and gathered his toiletries.

A knock at the door came sooner than he'd expected. He went to open it and saw that his reporter lady had already managed to throw her clothes on and yank the door open for the skinny bellboy. She slung her purse over her shoulder and moved quickly past him out into the hall. Agosto gestured toward the bags waiting on the bed. While the bellboy positioned them on his trolley, he followed her into the hallway.

"Thank you, Jane Goodall. I had a lovely time. Perhaps when I'm in town again…"

She flipped him her middle finger and stepped into the elevator.

He laughed softly and shook his head. American women.

The bellboy trailed him into the hall and stood attentively.

"I'll be downstairs in a minute. You can put those in the trunk of my car."

"Yes sir."

Inside the room, he dialed his assistant, explained where he was going and demanded everything would be ready when he got there. Handel might think he could control things for Margaret, protect her from the big bad wolf, but he'd just made the wolf very hungry.

***

"We need goats?" Billie repeated blankly. "Nubian goats? Whatever for?"

Margaret opened the folder she brought to the meeting and pulled out a magazine article she'd read. Her Internet research had also reinforced the idea in her mind. Goats could be tethered and allowed to feed on the weeds of the vineyard, cutting back even more the use of pesticides and herbicides. They already had the special tractor attachment Jack purchased before he died that gently moved between the vines, tilling the weeds back into the soil. The goats would take care of the weeds in between tilling.

Billie perused the article before handing it back, her brows lifted. "You're kidding, right?"

"No. I think they would completely negate our need of weed sprays, and being a greener business would put us in a position to…"

Billie cut her off. "It was a joke. Goats. Kids. Kidding. Get it?"

Sally, sitting across the conference table typing notes on her laptop, snorted. "If you have to explain it, it's not funny, boss."

Billie shot Sally a scathing look, then turned to Margaret. "Sorry. I'm not laughing at your idea. I think it's great. Just trying to bring a little levity into our day. *Some* people don't know humor when they hear it."

"Some people don't know humor," Sally muttered.

"Anyway, I'm definitely jumping on the green bandwagon. I don't think we'll survive long in California if we don't. Regulations seem to be on everything around here. So, if goats will help save the planet while weeding the vineyard, I'm all for it. Just make sure you name one of them *Sally*."

"Hey, I take offense at that!"

Margaret laughed at Sally's supposed outrage. She'd known her long enough to know that she'd probably be proud to have a goat named after her. "Fine with me. I'll look into buying them. You can name them."

Billie stood up and stretched. "We've tackled enough new business for now. I love your idea of wineblending. We have three varieties, two going back decades, and yet as far as I know Jack always harvested and crushed them separately. If we could come up with an old family wine recipe…wouldn't that be awesome? People like drinking a bit of history. It gives the wine respectability."

Sally broke out singing, "R-e-s-p-e-c-t…" and carried her computer from the conference room, swaying to the beat.

Margaret picked up her folder. "You know, my grandfather used an old wineblending recipe when he owned the winery. I think he got it from the previous owners. I know it must go way back before the property split. I remember my father talking about the formula when I was little."

"Before the property split?" Billie pushed her chair in and leaned her arms on the back. "What do you mean?"

"You didn't know?" She wondered how Handel could have left that little tidbit out of their conversations for the past eighteens months and whether he did it to protect her. He knew how much she loved the vineyard. But he couldn't possibly think Billie would try to take it from them. "Our three acres used to be part of the winery land. When my grandfather sold out, he managed to keep a plot for his family. My small vineyard contains some of the original vines from the forties."

"And you've been keeping that all to yourself?"

She shrugged. "I didn't know it was a secret. In fact, I'm sure the winery has records of the sale. There was some dispute about the acres we kept, but when Jack bought the winery, he let it go. He thought we'd been through enough I guess, without digging up ancient boundary lines and taking us to court over them."

Billie worried her bottom lip. "Jack did have a soft side for the underdog."

"I guess." Margaret moved toward the door. "I know I've just joined the team, but thanks for giving me the chance to prove myself. I won't let you down."

"I know you won't. You've already proven you know the winery business. Fredrickson's won't fail or succeed because of one person. It's like you said—we're a team." Billie followed her out the door and into the hallway. She linked arms with her as they strolled toward the front office. "By the way, what in the world did you do to my brother last night?"

Margaret cut a glance at her soon to be sister-in-law. "Do?" she blew out a nervous laugh and shrugged. "Nothing."

"Not what I heard." Billie led her past the office and out the front door, mercifully out of Sally's bionic hearing. She turned to face her, hands on narrow hips. "He raved about your cooking. To hear him tell it, you are the grill queen of California."

Margaret could feel heat flush her cheeks.

"He also said you make the best wine he's ever had. Which of course cinched the deal to hire you as our chief winemaker." She paused. "But I don't think it was the food or wine that made him come home singing, *This Kiss*. He doesn't even like country music."

"He did not!" Margaret knew her face was beet red. She looked away. "It was stupid. He's so young."

"Margaret, he's only two years younger than you. And he really likes you. There's nothing wrong with that. Enjoy it."

"I like him too. It's just that I come with excess baggage. Not that I consider Davy that way, but all the stuff that comes with having a child—including the father who recently showed up on my doorstep."

"I heard about that. What are you going to do?" Billie asked.

"I've gone over it in my mind a thousand times since I heard he was here. My first reaction was to deny him access to Davy. He didn't deserve it. For the past nine years he was the invisible father—never reached out to his son, wouldn't even acknowledge he was his son. Why now?" She released a sigh. "But then he came to see me yesterday. He seemed different, less cocky, maybe a little remorseful for the way he ran off." She shook her head slowly. "I don't know."

Billie reached out and gave her arm a gentle squeeze. "Well, call me when you do. I'm licensed to practice in California now. Family law is what I know. I dealt mostly with divorce, restraining orders against abusive husbands, that kind of thing, but I had a few child custody cases. They can be brutal. Believe me, you need a good lawyer. I know your brother probably thinks he can handle it, but he's much too close to the situation and it's not his specialty. So, don't hesitate to ask for help."

"Thanks." Her eyes welled with tears and she gave Billie a quick hug. "I'll let you know."

106

***

The telephone was ringing when she opened the door. The machine picked up before she could get to it. The caller I.D. number wasn't familiar, so she turned away and went to the refrigerator to see what to make for dinner. The prerecorded message played, followed by the beep.

"Hello, Margaret." Agosto's voice reverberated through the tiny speaker. She froze. "I didn't hear from you, so I decided to forge ahead. Davy and I are going to the park to play soccer. I'll bring him home around five-thirty. Talk to you then."

She slammed the door of the refrigerator shut and flew to the machine, lifted the receiver, "Agosto!" she yelled, but he'd already hung up. The dial tone droned like an angry bee. She dropped the phone, grabbed her keys from the table where she'd tossed them earlier and ran out to her car.

She heard the bus coming up the highway. Maybe Agosto was playing with her. Maybe he meant he'd pick up Davy and take him to the park to play soccer after he got off the bus. He couldn't have taken Davy from school. Wouldn't the teachers, the bus driver, someone, stop him, a stranger, from taking her son without permission?

She broke into a jog and got to the end of the driveway before the bus arrived. The engine didn't sound as though it were slowing down. Mr. Hadley nodded hello as he drove by, but when she waved her arms for him to stop, he didn't seem to notice.

Sweat broke out on her upper lip and she could feel blood pounding loudly in her ears. Davy was not on the bus. Agosto had taken him. Where? She ran back toward the house. He said they were going to the park to play soccer, but how could she know for sure he was telling the truth? And which park? The one by Davy's school?

She rubbed her hands over her face and tried to think. This couldn't be happening. Davy was taught never to get into a car with a stranger. Why would he go with Agosto? He'd never met him or even seen a picture of him. She turned and ran back to the car, climbed in and started the engine, then shut it off. Where would she go?

Handel would know what to do. He always knew what to do. She jerked the door open and ran back into the house to retrieve her cell phone. She dumped her purse out on the table before she found it in the side pocket, pushed Handel's quick dial number and waited, biting her lip and praying Davy was all right.

"Margaret?"

"Handel, he took him! He took Davy!" She began to sob uncontrollably. She heard him say something but couldn't understand.

"Margaret!" Handel finally shouted into the phone. "Who took Davy? Get a hold of yourself and tell me what's going on. I can't help if you don't…"

"Agosto," she managed to say, his name like a curse word grating on her tongue. She wiped at her face with the sleeve of her t-shirt, stammering an explanation. "He called to say he took Davy from school. To play soccer. Said they were going to a park. That he'd bring him home at 5:30." She sniffed and tried to breathe, but her chest hurt at the simple action. Was she having a heart attack or was the thought of life without Davy so horrendous to cause her heart to physically ache?

"Calm down. He said he would bring him home. That's good."

Handel's calm and collected attitude grated on her already prickly nerves. "That's good? The man kidnaps my son and you say its good?"

"Hold on. Call the school and find out if Davy's still there. If he's not—call the police and report him missing. I want this on that bastard's record. He can't come here and act like he has rights. The court system won't acknowledge him as the father since his name is not on the birth certificate. So, until he rectifies that by going to court with a paternity suit, he's just a kidnapper."

"Why would Davy go with him?" she asked, not expecting an answer but unable to stop the questions, the finger pointing back at her. If only she'd talked to her son about his father. Maybe none of this would be happening.

"Margaret," Handel repeated sternly. "Call the school and the police. I'll be home as soon I can. I'm leaving now."

***

The officer listened to the message on the machine and wrote something in his notebook. He looked up, his eyes taking in Margaret's purse dumped out on the table where she'd searched for her phone, the tear tracks in her makeup, and the bottle of wine and empty glass on the kitchen cupboard. She'd needed a drink while she waited. It probably looked bad—drinking when her son was missing—but she had been shaking so hard and she didn't know what to do.

"Doesn't sound like a kidnapping, ma'am," he said. He flipped his notebook shut and slid it in his front shirt pocket. His expression was bland, but his tone conveyed skepticism. "This man—what is his relationship to your son?"

"There is no relationship. Davy has never seen him before. He's a complete stranger to my son!"

"Then why would he take him to play soccer?" He hooked his thumbs in his belt and cocked his head to the side, like a bird alert for signs of emerging worms.

She threw up her hands. "I don't know! I haven't seen him for over ten years. Suddenly he's back in town and wants to see Davy."

"So he is the boy's father," he said, his lips thinned into a straight line. "Does he have visitation rights?"

"No! He has absolutely no rights. He left the country when I was pregnant. He's never seen my son, or spoken to him. Is that clear enough for you? The man is not Davy's father. He's a deadbeat sperm donor." She crossed her arms and bit back the rest of the diatribe that wanted to flood out of her mouth. The officer looked like he'd enjoy arresting her for a smart mouth.

She heard Handel come through the garage door, his shoes clicking on the ceramic tile. He put his arm around her as he calmly took in the situation. He held out his hand to the officer. "I'm Handel Parker, Davy's uncle. Have you issued an Amber alert? I didn't hear one on the radio. Time is of the essence. Agosto Salvatore is Italian. He could possibly be planning to take Davy out of the country."

The officer's gaze narrowed. "I don't think it will come to that. Mr. Salvatore left a message on your sister's machine that stated exactly what time he would bring his son home. Perhaps your sister has forgotten that they had a date," he said.

"What are you implying?" she demanded. "Do you really think that I would forget something like that?"

He inclined his head toward the bottle on the cabinet. "You have been drinking, Ms. Parker."

Handel stopped her arm when she would have taken a swing at the officer. "Margaret, please find a photo of Davy for the officer," he said firmly. He didn't let go until she nodded, her muscles going slack.

"I don't think that's necessary," said the officer. "I'm sure…"

"I don't think you understand the situation. A man took my nephew without permission. This man's name is not on the birth certificate. He has absolutely no legal standing to go near my nephew. As an officer it is your sworn duty to uphold the law. My nephew has been taken. He is nine years old. He has blonde hair and blue eyes. His name is Davy Handel Parker. If you want to keep your job working for the citizens of this county I strongly urge you to issue an Amber alert." He handed the officer his business card and calmly waited for a response.

Margaret never left the room but only moved to the bulletin board beside the refrigerator and took down the photo of Davy she'd pinned to the cork board just the week before. It was taken in the vineyard, in the heat of the afternoon, his bare chest tan from running around outside without a shirt, his blonde hair even whiter than normal, bleached in the summer sun.

She moved back to Handel's side and extended the photo to the officer.

He nodded curtly, and stepped out to his car to radio it in.

"Are they going to look for him?" she asked, glancing up at the clock on the wall. It was 4:58 already. If Agosto had been telling the truth, Davy would be home in thirty-two minutes. If he wasn't…

"I'm sure Agosto will bring him home before Officer Starchy-pants condescends to uphold the law." He stepped to the window and watched the policeman sitting in his car talking on the radio. "I'd bet money that man is going through a custody battle of his own right now. But I don't care if his ex-wife took the kids, the dog, and his last can of beer, if his negligence is the cause of Agosto taking Davy out of this country, I will put this county through such a mudslide of law suits, they won't be able to crawl out for a hundred years."

She couldn't help smiling at his vendetta lawyer talk. Handel, the one who taught Davy, when a bigger kid was picking on him at school, that revenge made a man weak, while forgiveness took a man's power back from the bully. She knew he was just being protective and feeling inadequate—as she was. The court system was fine revenge after the fact, but right now they needed real action.

The officer returned, his face a mask of official business. "Do either of you know what type of vehicle Mr. Salvatore was driving?" he asked.

"Yes." Relief slipped through her veins at the thought that authorities would soon be looking for her son. "He came here a couple days ago in a blue convertible sports car. It was expensive. I think it might have been a Ferrari. I didn't see it up close."

His eyes widened at the description. He nodded. "All right. We already have patrols doing drive-bys of the parks in the area." He handed her his card. "Call me if he shows up."

"Thank you, Officer Tate. I'm sorry I lost my temper. He's the only son I have."

The corners of his mouth relented and curved up slightly. "I understand."

***

Handel was first out the door when the convertible pulled up to the house. He didn't wait for Agosto to get out of the car, but leaned over the door and pulled him up by the collar of his shirt. The man hung there, choking against the tightened fabric until Handel released him and slammed him back down into the seat. "You dirty…"

"Handel!" Margaret caught up to him and grabbed his arm before he could do worse. "Not like this," she warned, even though every instinct screamed to hit the man herself. But Davy was sitting in the passenger seat, his eyes as round as quarters, and she didn't want to scare him more than he already was.

"Davy, get out of the car," Handel ordered.

Davy opened the door timidly as though he expected the same treatment himself. She didn't wait for him to come to her but flew around the front of the car and wrapped her arms around his small frame. "You scared me to death," she breathed into his hair. He smelled of sweat and riding in the open wind and she hugged him hard, relief swelling her heart.

"Mom," he said, pulling back, "you're choking me."

He was home safe and she was suddenly furious. She straightened, hands on her hips. "I'll do worse than that if you ever get into a stranger's car again. Now get in the house and take a shower. I'll be there in a minute."

"He said you'd be mad at me," Davy said, in a persecuted tone. "But he's not a stranger and you know it."

The words sent a chill down her spine. Agosto had already taken a bit of the respect and trust her son had

114

in her and destroyed it with his version of the truth. She pointed at the house and Davy reluctantly obeyed.

As soon as he went inside, Handel yanked open the car door and pulled Agosto from the seat. "I warned you ten years ago that if you ever came back, your life wouldn't be worth a bullet to take it."

Agosto jerked away, his handsome face twisted with rage. "How dare you touch me. I will have you arrested for assault. You may be a lawyer but you are not above the law."

"You first. The police have already issued a warrant for your arrest, for kidnapping my nephew. Did you account for that scenario in your plan?"

Agosto turned to Margaret, a look of astonishment drawing his brows together. "Why would you do that? You knew I just took him to play soccer. I would never hurt my own son. Do you hate me that much?" he asked, wounded regret creeping into his voice.

"Don't even start with me," she said, moving around the car to stand beside Handel. "Against my brother's advice, I considered allowing you some sort of relationship with my son, and you've thrown that tiny bit of trust that had begun to sprout, back in my face, by taking him without permission and without my knowledge." She pointed her finger at him, her hand shaking with pent-up fury and overwhelming relief. "You will never have anything to do with Davy again as long as I live!"

Agosto stared back at her, then calmly moved around them both and climbed into the car, slamming the door. He twisted the key in the ignition before looking up, dark glasses now hiding his emotions. "I actually thought that perhaps you and I could start over. Learn to care for one another once again. Raise our son together as a family. But you've destroyed that dream." He slipped the car into reverse. "You will be hearing from my lawyers," he said, leaving them with a dismissive wave of his manicured hand.

Margaret grabbed Handel's arm and held on. To keep him from going after the man or to keep herself from screaming, she didn't know. Gravel dust hung in the air in the wake of Agosto's departure like poison fumes from a chemical spill.

"I think you made him angry," Handel noted, a satisfied lilt to his words.

She breathed out a laugh based purely on frayed nerves. "Me? You're the one who wrinkled his two hundred dollar polo shirt. He's probably talking to his lawyers about it right now." The fact that Davy was home, safe and sound, made her giddy with relief. She knew she shouldn't be relieved quite yet. Agosto was obviously serious about pursuing his paternity rights in court, but right now all she could think about was what to make Davy for dinner. There would be time for admonitions and courtroom strategy later. Right now she wanted to lavish her son with love and pizza.

CHAPTER NINE

"Just as I thought. He didn't spend five minutes in jail. Apparently, his father's wealth and influence extends to our little neck of the woods. His lawyers have been busy. They've already filed a paternity case to get the blood work flowing. With Salvatore's ego, he'll be filing for sole custody next."

Margaret sighed. She switched the phone to her left ear as she listened. "I hope you're not saying that's even possible."

"He can ask all he wants, but ten years without support or acknowledgment of any kind, in the eyes of the law, looks rather poor for his case."

"Handel," she began hesitantly, "I've spoken with Billie about handling this. She is a family lawyer and knows what to expect. And I think you are too close to be objective."

"I'm perfectly capable of…"

"You verbally threatened Agosto and physically assaulted him. In front of Davy, no less. I know you want to help, but I think you need to keep your distance on this one. It's for the best. For all of us."

He was silent a moment. "You're right," he said finally, his voice heavy with wounds deeper than time could heal. "Davy hasn't looked at me the same since. It's like he's afraid of me. I turned into a monster right in front of him and he doesn't know when that monster will resurface again. The way I felt when dad…"

"Handel, don't! You are not anything like him. You have done nothing but love and care for us since he left. I'm only asking you to step back because I don't want to see your reputation and career ruined. This is my chance to do something for you. I need you to understand."

"All right. I'll hand everything over to Billie this afternoon."

"Thank you."

"Margaret?" he said, before she could disconnect. "I want you to know that I will do anything it takes to keep that man away from you and Davy. Anything."

She set the phone on the counter and stared unblinkingly out the window, seeing only the murderous look on Handel's face when he pulled Agosto from the car.

Anything. That's what she was afraid of.

***

"But why can't I see my dad?" Davy asked again, watching her for signs of weakness like when she said "no ice cream before dinner" and he begged until she gave in.

Ruining his dinner once in a while was a small concession to day-to-day rules. Ruining his life was another matter altogether. Agosto's idea of fatherhood did not include love and nurture. She doubted he even knew the definition for them. The stories he had told her about the senior Mr. Salvatore made her wonder if the man cared more about his fine stable and gave more thought to raising expensive race horses than raising his son. Agosto at twenty was skewed by his father's inattention. Ten years later she doubted he had changed for the better.

"Davy," she said, trying once again to make him understand. "He is your biological father—not your dad. A dad is there when you're born. He helps raise you, gives hugs and high fives, teaches kindness and forgiveness. How to work hard. To be responsible." She smiled. "He even cleans up after you when you have the flu. A dad sticks around for all of those things. Agosto Salvatore is not your dad."

Davy bit at the inside of his jaw while he digested her latest explanation. "A dad is a lot like Uncle Handel," he said finally.

She pushed his hair back out of his face. "Yes. Uncle Handel did all the things a real dad would do. You might say he was a pinch-hitter dad."

He grinned at that analogy. "Uncle Handel hates baseball."

119

"I know, but he always went to your t-ball games and cheered, didn't he?"

"But my bilogic father said he wants to take me to Italy to visit my other grandfather. And he has a horse for me. I'd like to have a horse. Wouldn't that be cool?" He picked up a banana. "Can I have this? I'm hungry."

She nodded and watched him peel the top down and take a bite. Hunger always trumped angst. "I'm sure a horse would be cool, but Italy is very, very far away. Across the ocean. Too far away for a boy to travel without his mother. I'd be awfully lonely without you."

"Are you afraid my other grandfather is bad like Grandpa Sean?" he asked, calmly chewing banana as though every kid had a grandpa in prison.

"No," she said, her throat tightening, "I don't think he's like Grandpa Sean. I just want to spend all the time I can with you before you grow up and leave for college."

"That's silly. I'm only nine," he said, grinning.

"Yeah, but you're really smart. One of those colleges might want to take you early."

He shook his head and threw the banana peel in the garbage. "Nope. I'm going to be a wine vintner and master wine maker. I don't need to go to college for that. You didn't."

"You might change your mind. Remember last week you wanted to be a professional soccer player, and about a month ago you wanted to be an astronaut."

"I guess. I'll think about it."

"Glad to hear it. You've got eight years to mull it over. Now go outside and play till I call you for dinner."

He picked up his ball and opened the door.

"Stay close to the house though, okay?" she added. "No running off to Billie's tonight."

He grunted and pulled the door closed behind him.

She went to the window and watched him kick the ball up and down the driveway, his tongue protruding between his lips whenever he tried to balance it on his knee or bounce it off his head. He was wearing that blasted cap again—the one from the racetrack that Agosto gave him on their little outing—probably why he was having such a hard time directing the ball with his head. She smiled when she realized he was wearing two different colors of socks. His jeans were getting too short. He must have grown an inch since school started. They would need to go shopping again soon. Otherwise everyone would think her son was colorblind.

She wished she didn't feel paranoid every time he played outside alone. Last year when her father ran loose in the neighborhood, terrorizing Billie and avoiding the authorities, she refused to let Davy play outside for weeks. After he was returned to prison, she'd felt immense relief and her sense of safety gradually returned. Now with Agosto threatening to take her son, she wanted to lock Davy in his room. But she knew he needed continuity. She didn't want him living a life of fear.

She moved away from the window. She couldn't stand and watch him every minute. This was crazy. Agosto was going through the court system. She had no reason to think he would break the law by coming on her property again. Billie had filed a restraining order against him to keep him at bay. When the court system ruled against him…that's when she would need to worry.

In the family room, she picked up a magazine and stretched out on the couch to read. But all she saw was her father's weathered, craggy face, the last time she saw him. She still couldn't wrap her mind around the facts. She was shocked to learn her father was not just a drunk who had deserted his family, but a cold, calculated, child molester. It made her feel tainted as though his actions somehow corrupted her soul as well. She imagined some people saw her that way. She'd seen the looks, heard whispered remarks behind her back. They thought she was another one of her father's victims. Thank God she had been spared. She'd only been four years old when he disappeared all those years ago, and before that, Handel protected her, a flesh and bone shield. She realized now that even as a boy he took beatings meant for their mother, tried to direct Sean Parker's anger toward himself until the man was spent and passed out drunk. She owed her brother a lot.

She threw the magazine down and sat up. She couldn't concentrate. She had to stay busy. Keep her mind occupied with something other than the past.

Adam's guitar was still propped against the table. She leaned over and picked it up, held it in her lap and ran her fingers over the strings. How would it feel to play with that much passion? He had a gift. She set it gently on the couch beside her and reached out for the phone on the coffee table. She dialed the number and listened to it ring five times before he picked up.

He was breathing hard like he'd run in from outside. "Hello?"

"Hello," she said, and then couldn't think of a thing to say.

"Meg?"

She smiled against the receiver. "Who said you could give me a nickname?" she asked.

"You didn't mind the other night. Just seeing if it stuck."

"Handel's not even allowed to shorten my name."

"I'm not Handel," he said, his voice deep and confident.

"Well, I called to remind you that your guitar's still here." She smoothed a hand over the worn fabric of the couch, cringing inwardly at her feeble excuse.

He laughed. "It better still be there. Cause I haven't come to fetch it home yet."

"Sounds like a pet."

"Meg. I love my guitar. I don't leave it behind at just anybodies house."

Margaret couldn't believe she was having this conversation. She hadn't flirted with a guy for the sake of flirting since she was a teenager. It made her feel young and carefree again. She heard the kitchen door slam shut and a ball bounce against the tile floor. Davy was back. She jumped up. Not as carefree as imagined.

"I have to go. Come by this evening and I might let you have it back." She didn't wait for a response but pushed the end button and set the phone on the table.

"Mom!" Davy yelled from the kitchen when she didn't materialize immediately.

"In here."

He followed the sound of her voice, gently kicking the ball down the hall and into the room. He tapped it with his toe and caught it in his arms, grinning. "Cool, huh?"

"I thought I told you not to play with the ball in the house."

"I was careful."

"That's not the point," she said, taking it from him and holding it over her head. "Now it's mine, soccer boy," she teased.

He tried to jump and knock it from her hand, but she managed to keep it just out of his reach. "Oh no you don't!"

"Hey, that's not fair. You're taller than me." He slumped into an overstuffed chair and crossed his arms, his pout reminding her of Agosto.

"Tell you what. You can have it back after you clean your room."

"Ahh, Mom. Do I got to? I like it just the way it is."

She laughed and pulled him up. "The funny thing about that is, your room never stays just the way it is. It continues to get worse and worse. So, let's nip that in the bud, shall we?"

"All right, " he said, but his tone implied it was totally against everything he stood for. Mostly—freedom to have a messy room. He trudged off, making it look like he was headed for the guillotine. He stopped and looked back, a puzzled frown on his face. "When did Grandpa Sean get out of jail?" he asked.

She dropped the ball. It rolled under the coffee table and over to the piano. "What do you mean?" she asked, trepidation pulling at her like a rip current.

"I saw him out in the vineyard," Davy stated matter-of-factly. "I think he came out of your storage shed."

"Storage shed?"

He shrugged. "I don't know. He was over by it."

"Did you speak to him?" she asked, hoping it was only boyhood imagination.

He shook his head. "You told me not to."

Margaret gestured for him to get a move on. "Good. Now get your room clean."

When he was out of sight, she sat down on the edge of the couch and dropped her head in her hands. Was it possible that he'd been released from prison without any notification for the family? Handel would have called. He certainly would have let Billie know. What was going on?

She hurried to the kitchen and checked that the garage door was down and the inside door locked. Then did the same for the front door. Her father was not supposed to get out of prison for years. They had all hoped parole would be denied him, many times over. He was a dangerous man and she didn't want Davy anywhere near him.

She peered out the kitchen window toward the vineyard, squinting against the afternoon sun. What was he doing here? Was he looking for something, or just returning to the scene of his many crimes?

***

Handel called back later that afternoon. He was in San Francisco, going through jury selection for an upcoming trial. He expected to drive home in the morning after rush hour traffic. He couldn't get back any sooner, but he'd made some calls in advance.

"The parole board actually stated that they believe he's on his way to complete rehabilitation and should be given a chance to prove his worth to society." He blew out a frustrated breath. "Apparently, he's been an exemplary prisoner, and it didn't hurt his case that the prison is full to overflowing. But most surprisingly, he had two upstanding citizens speak out on his behalf. I don't know who they were, but I'm going to find out."

Her brother was naturally concerned for Billie. He would be calling her after he got off the phone. He urged her to be careful and keep Davy inside after dark.

As if she had any intention of letting him out of her sight. "Don't worry about us. Tell Billie to be careful. She's the one he threatened."

The phone rang right after she hung up. She picked up immediately, assuming he'd forgotten to tell her something. "Handel?"

"No," a gruff voice answered, "This is your father." He coughed and it sounded like he was going to hack up a lung. "Don't hang up. I need to talk to you."

"You don't have anything to say that I want to hear," she said, her voice tight with anger. How dare he call after all he put them through? Last time he showed up she begged Handel to give him a chance, and she'd lived with regret ever since.

"Maggie. You don't mean that."

She tensed at the childhood name. Her mother had called her, Maggie. When she died, no one was allowed to use that name again. Especially not the man who made her mother's life miserable to the end. "I do mean that. Don't call here again," she said and slammed the phone down.

Tears slid down her cheeks and she brushed them away with angry movements, unwilling to acknowledge the reason she cried. Not for herself. Her father had never been a dad. She was used to it.

Seconds later, the phone rang again. And rang and rang. Then she disconnected it from the wall.

***

Adam knocked on the door again. Margaret must be home. Handel said he'd talked to her earlier. He knocked harder and pressed the doorbell three times for good measure. "Meg!" he called out, stepping back to look up at the windows, all suspiciously shut against the cool of the evening. "Meg, are you there? Answer me!"

He heard movement behind the door and then the deadbolt clicked back and the door was pulled open. "Hey, Adam. What are you yelling about?" Davy asked, rubbing his eyes. "You woke me up."

"Sorry, pal. Where's your mom?" he asked, more worried now than before. Margaret would never leave Davy alone with Sean Parker running loose in the neighborhood.

He yawned widely, his eyes watering with the effort. "Don't know. Maybe she's in the cellar."

"You have a cellar?"

"Sure. I'll show you." He stood back and waited for Adam to enter before carefully closing the door and flipping the deadbolt. Then he looked up, his expression pensive. "Mom said to always lock the door. Grandpa Sean got out of jail."

Adam patted him on the back. "Good job. Show me where the cellar is and you can get back to bed."

Davy trudged in bare feet down the hall, through the kitchen, and out the service door to the garage. He pointed to the far corner. A slanting wooden door was propped open over a descending flight of stone steps. Yellow tinged light gleamed from the opening. "She's down there," he said. He yawned again. "Can I go back to bed now?"

Adam ruffled the boy's hair. "Yeah, sure. Sorry for waking you up."

Davy shuffled sleepily off to his room and Adam moved toward the cellar door. He heard music floating up the stairs, faint and crackily from a radio station with bad reception. An oldies station was playing *Please Mr. Postman*—Karen Carpenter's voice smooth and creamy as new butter. Then Meg sang along, so far off key it was practically a different song. He covered his laugh with a fake coughing fit and she jerked around with an empty bottle raised over her head.

He dodged to the right. "Hey! It's me. Careful with that thing. I have a soft skull."

She blew out a relieved breath and set the bottle down on a low table. "Do you have to keep sneaking up on me all the time? I'm too young for a heart attack."

"Sorry." He grinned at the picture she made. With a white lab coat buttoned up over her clothes, and her blonde hair pulled into two ponytails high on the sides of her head, she looked like Chrissy on Three's Company doing a parody of The Nutty Professor.

"How'd you get in anyway?" she asked, moving toward the stairs.

"Don't worry. The front door is locked. Davy let me in and went back to bed."

She was obviously relieved. "Good. Not that you woke him up, but that he went back to bed. I was worried he wouldn't sleep after this afternoon." She moved to the table where she had bunches of grapes and some testing equipment spread out. Behind her, a press and another machine he didn't recognize, filled half the room. Four small oak barrels, two on each side of a narrow doorway, were most likely last year's wine still going through fermentation.

"What are you up to?" he asked, stepping closer to watch.

"I'm testing the level of acidity. Ripe grapes should be between 0.58 and 0.64. These are showing 0.59," she said looking up with a pleased expression. "This is going to be one busy week. Thankfully, I've talked Billie into a joint venture, now that I'm her chief winemaker. I'd never have time to harvest my own vineyard, otherwise. We're going to add a new wine to Fredrickson's list. A field blend. I found a very old wineblending recipe that belonged to my grandfather. The Parker vineyard was planted with half a dozen different kinds of grapes back in the forty's. It was once actually part of Fredrickson's. I think with a couple added varietals from Fredrickson's newer vines, we will have something uniquely special." She moved away from the table and disappeared through the narrow stone doorway, but soon returned with a bottle of wine in hand, and continued. "Field blending is an art form that's nearly disappeared around here. Most wine made in Napa is from single grape dedicated, homogenous vineyards. But we are going retro!"

"Cool." He reached out, plucked a grape, and popped it in his mouth. "Do you get top billing too?" he asked.

"She did say I could name it. But I suppose I'll have to come up with something new." She set the dusty bottle down, and wiped it off with a nearby towel. The label said, *Margaret's Wine*.

He took it from her hand to get a better look. "Hmm. I would have called it, Meg's Brew."

"Wine isn't brewed—beer is," she said, unbuttoning her lab coat. "With your lack of knowledge for this business, you may not even last as the accountant."

"That's harsh."

"Let's get out of here." She clicked off the radio.

He carried the wine, and she closed and locked the wine cellar door behind them. The house was quiet when they slipped in. "I just want to check on Davy," she said, leaving him in the kitchen while she climbed the stairs to her son's room.

He rummaged around for a corkscrew and glasses. Managed to find both before she returned. "Is he sleeping?" he asked, smoothly pulling the cork from the bottle.

"Yeah. He's fine. I'm the one who seems to have a problem sleeping nights. First, Agosto comes back and rips a hole in my little world with his demand for joint custody of Davy, and now my father returns. I may never sleep again." She took the glass of wine he held out, her hand shaking slightly.

"You want to sit outside?" he asked. "It's a beautiful night."

The patio was awash with the glow of the full moon. He pulled another chair close to hers and set the bottle on the table within reach. Crickets chirped somewhere behind the grill and a light breeze ruffled leaves on nearby oaks. The whine of a small bi-plane sounded overhead, tiny lights twinkling against the black velvet expanse.

He was quiet, letting her unwind while they sipped wine and listened to the sounds of the night. Slowly he reached out and laced her fingers with his and let them rest on the arm of her chair. She turned her face toward him and smiled.

"I'm sorry about giving you a hard time about being too young," she said. "It's just that sometimes I feel like someone borrowed years of my life and never returned them. I don't want that to happen to you."

"Are you talking about Davy?"

"Don't get me wrong. I regret my affair with Agosto ten years ago. I don't regret having Davy. Well," she shrugged, "sometimes when he's driving me crazy, but all Mother's feel that—don't they?"

"You're a great mom and Davy's a great kid. Things will work out. I have total confidence in my sister's attorney skills. When it comes to fighting for the underdog, she is in there tooth and nail."

"I'm sure you're right," she said, but there was a lack of confidence in her voice.

"By the way, I heard through the grapevine that your old flame actually suggested he was willing to start over. I'm glad you didn't jump at the chance."

She breathed out a faint laugh and shook her head. "Yeah, like that's gonna happen. He was only trying to manipulate me. I find it very hard to believe he could ever learn to love anyone but himself."

"The first time I saw him I thought—Hollywood."

"What?"

"You know—the perfect leading man in a chick flick. Handsome, well-groomed, knows how to speak Italian."

She took a sip of wine, her eyes sparkling with laughter.

"You two would never work out. You need someone down to earth, with an ego that doesn't overpower the relationship. Someone like me. An average, hard-working guy with open arms and a heart as big as Yankee Stadium. I'm your Joe Demaggio."

She burst out laughing. "Right. And we know how well that turned out."

He shrugged. "Well, I'm not exactly like Joe Demaggio. I'm better looking. More like Joe Mauer."

"And how is *your* ego going to stay under control?" she teased, holding her glass out for a refill.

He took the bottle from the table and leaned toward her to fill her glass. "I'm sure you'll think of a way," he said. "My ego's already been knocked down a few pegs since I met you. What about that first day I knocked on your door?"

She groaned and covered her face with one hand. "Don't remind me. Sometimes I can be a real…"

"Hey!" he interrupted, "Don't be so hard on yourself. I deserved it. I was insensitive, immature, and probably smelled like a gymnasium after walking for an hour in the sun. I don't blame you for not seeing the real me under all that raw masculinity."

She made a sound of disbelief. "That's amazing. You managed to turn an apology of sorts into a bragathon."

He gulped the rest of the wine in his glass and set it on the table. "Believe me, it's a special skill I don't take lightly." He took her glass and set it beside him, then pulled her to her feet. "My other skills could use practice though," he said and bent his head to kiss her.

"Get away from my daughter!" a smoke-filled voice crackled like sparks from a bonfire as a tall, dark figure separated from the shadow of the trees and advanced toward them. "You're another damn Fredrickson, come to take what don't belong to you," he accused. Ten paces away, he stopped and took a drag on the cigarette he held. Smoke exited his nose and wreathed his head momentarily, appearing like an unstable halo in the glow of the moon. He dropped the nub and crushed it with the heel of his boot, never taking his eyes from Adam.

Adam stepped between Margaret and her father, his hands clenched at his sides. Just the thought of what this man did to his sister was enough to churn his gut with blind rage. "I think you better leave before I finish what those cigarettes only started."

Sean Parker laughed, a harsh sound of lung damage and age. "Believe me, boy, many have tried before you, but none have succeeded. Why don't you run on home now so I can talk to my baby girl."

Margaret pressed her hand against Adam's back and slowly moved past him. "It's all right," she whispered close to his ear. She took two steps toward her father and stopped. "What do you want?" Her voice was brittle as toffee at shattering stage. "Haven't you done enough damage to our family?"

Sean Parker coughed and spat on the ground. He casually pushed his hands in the front pockets of his jeans and looked at her like a wayward child. "Maggie, you know I'd never hurt you or Davy. I've done my time and I'm going straight. I just need a helping hand. We are family."

Adam could see her tense, her back straightening like a soldier with orders. "We are not family. And for the record, the rest of your life wouldn't have been enough time to pay back what you took from those children, from my mother and from Handel." With each word her voice strengthened. She stepped forward and pointed her finger in her father's face. "As far as this family is concerned, you died a long time ago. Now get off my property or I will file charges against you myself!"

His eyes narrowed and his lips hardened into the angry man he'd become. "Handel's turned you against me. He's always been soft. If he were the Parker I raised him to be he would have found a way by now to use that fancy law degree to take back what's ours."

"Thank God he isn't like you. You are a hateful, destructive man," her words were but a breath on the wind.

Adam could tell she was about ready to have an emotional meltdown. He stepped up and drew her into his arms, turning her face away from Sean Parker. "Go inside and call the police. I'll stay and make sure he leaves."

She hesitated, then pulled away and without looking back made her way across the patio.

Sean laughed. The dry cackle reminded Adam of a crow's harsh cry in a Minnesota winter. "Maggie, I know what you and Handel are trying to do, sleeping with the opposition, but marrying the bastards is a tough way to get your inheritance back," he called after her.

She paused with her hand on the sliding door.

"I'm not asking for my share—just a few thousand to tide me over till I find a good job. Handel owes me that much after testifying against his own father."

Margaret turned back, her features etched like marble. "Go to hell," she said in a voice with enough heat to send him on his way. She slid the door open and disappeared inside.

Sean Parker turned his eyes on Adam and spit on the ground. "You tell her I'll be back. This isn't over," he said.

"You come back and I'll end it myself." Adam promised.

The old man smirked and walked off around the house toward the road.

Adam followed, keeping his distance. A sickening anger built stone upon stone inside of him until it became an altar of fury. If Sean Parker had made one wrong move or said one more thing, he would have been on him like a rabid animal, beating, kicking, clawing him to pieces in retribution for all he'd done. Thankfully, he didn't get his chance. The man climbed into an old pickup hiding in the trees at the end of the road and drove off. Adam watched the taillights disappear into the curve of the dark highway before running back up the drive and into the house.

Margaret was bent over the kitchen table, a metal lockbox open before her. She looked up at the sound of his step. Her face was wet with tears and there was a gun in her hands. She was trying to load it, unaccustomed fingers fumbling with bullets. She sniffed and wiped at her face with the back of her hand. "Is he gone?" she asked.

"Yes."

"We'll never be free of him until he's dead," she whispered.

The anger that burned so intensely in his chest now dissipated at sight of her desperation. "You don't mean that."

He stepped close and put his hand over hers, pointing the barrel downward. Her fingers were tense and cold as the black handgun. He gently pulled it from her grip and set it on the table. She released the bullets from her other hand, letting them drop back into the box, the sound like hail on a tin roof. He slowly drew her into his arms and she pressed her face against his chest, her tears dampening his t-shirt. She sobbed and shook and he held her there, never wanting to let go. In that moment he knew he would do anything to keep her safe.

CHAPTER TEN

"What do you mean, you can't? I have paid you an exorbitant amount of money to accelerate the process. I want to take my son home to Italy by the end of this month. Don't tell me it's not possible. Just do it!" He flipped the cell phone closed and laid it on the table beside him.

Carl's restaurant was already busy and bustling at five p.m. He still hadn't become accustomed to the seven and a half hour time difference from Rome, but he'd skipped lunch and he was starving. A waiter moved smoothly between tables offering free samples of a local Merlot. He waved him away when he neared his table. The man moved off to a rowdy group of middle-aged patrons, already half drunk from touring wineries.

Agosto picked up his glass of wine and took a sip. Letting it linger on his tongue, he breathed deeply. He detected a hint of nutmeg and lush, dark blackberries. There was a nose of cocoa and something else he couldn't quite...

"Agosto. I didn't know you were here." Carl stood beside him still in his chef coat, a puzzled look on his face. He eyed the bottle of wine on the table. "I see you've discovered Margaret's Wine."

"Please have a seat and share a glass with me." Agosto motioned for his cousin to sit. "If you can spare a few moments from your precious kitchen. We've hardly spoken since I've been back."

Carl turned toward the kitchen and nodded at a busboy standing there. The young man disappeared through the swinging doors. "I can sit for a minute." He took a wineglass from the unoccupied table next to them, pulled out a chair and sat, his face a mask of politeness.

"I suppose you know that Margaret has refused to allow me contact with my own son." He swallowed the rest of the wine in his glass and reached for the bottle. He refilled his and Carl's as well. "I thought perhaps we could start over. But she won't give me a chance."

"Did you really think that taking Davy was a good way to start over?" Carl asked, his tone sharp. "I find that hard to believe. You were always a conniving..."

Agosto put out his hand. "Stop right there! You have no right. It's been ten years since I was the boy you so despised. I'm a different man now. Am I to be punished for the rest of my life for an immature choice I made a decade ago?" He rubbed his hands over his face and sat back with a weary sigh. "I know I shouldn't have taken him. It was stupid. I waited for Margaret to call and she didn't. I wanted to see my son. To talk with him. To spend time with him as a father. So I took him—to play soccer. What is so horrible about that?" He shook his head. "She actually called the police."

Carl watched him as though he were a criminal on the witness stand. "What did you think she was going to do? Welcome you back with open arms? Handel and Margaret are my friends—my family. If you have any intention of hurting them again, you will answer to me this time."

"After all my father did for you," Agosto said. "He helped set you up in this restaurant, paid the loans you were unable to meet, and now you treat your family like this."

"I've paid my debt to your father. I do not owe one to you." Carl stood and pushed the chair carefully in, smoothing the white tablecloth in place. He lifted his glass and drained it in one gulp. "Thanks for the wine," he said, and walked away.

Agosto drew a deep breath and slowly released it. He smiled and sipped his wine, unconcerned by his cousin's warning. Carl had always been easy to lie to. He liked to take people at their word. He truly believed there was good in everyone, and given a chance they would do the right thing. That's really what his little warning was all about. Carl was giving him another chance to prove his worth. He laughed softly and reached out for the breadbasket.

***

The restaurant parking lot was well lit, but he didn't notice the man hunched inside the old pickup next to his car until he squeezed between the vehicles to open the door. The man climbed out and leaned with his forearms on the side panel of the pickup bed, staring boldly across at Agosto while he tried to open his door without banging it against the rust bucket beside him. He'd bought another bottle of Margaret's Wine to take back to the hotel and he carefully placed it on the seat before turning to face the man watching him.

"Could you perhaps move your truck so I can get into my car? It's much too close," he said, his words only slightly slurred. He knew he could get back to the hotel without mishap but backing up with an inch to spare might be a problem. The rental was extremely expensive and although it was well worth it, he didn't want to pay for damages that could have been avoided.

The man wore a faded baseball cap pulled low over his eyes and a couple days growth of grey whiskers covered his face like heavy sandpaper. He had a lit cigarette between his lips. He didn't bother to take it out, but spoke around it. "So you're Davy's daddy," he drawled, his voice as rough as his appearance. "I pictured someone a little different. More manly."

Agosto shut the door and turned to face the man. "Should I know you?" he asked, his eyes narrowed.

The man laughed. "No reason you should."

There was something about him that seemed familiar but Agosto knew he'd never laid eyes on him before. Even so, he felt the urge to escape back inside the restaurant. Instead, he opened his jacket, took out a cigarette, put it between his lips and lit it.

"I hear you had a little run-in with my Maggie." The man continued, as though they were in the middle of a normal conversation. "Lately, she seems to be channeling her momma—a harridan if there ever was one." He paused, took the cigarette from his lips and crushed it out in the bed of the pickup. "I can help you with that."

Agosto blew out a puff of smoke. Now he knew who the man was. The perfect patsy.

***

The winery was alive with activity at two a.m. Margaret surveyed the pickup trucks filled with empty crates, tools, and water tanks for the workers. Everything seemed to be ready. Harvesting the grapes in the cool of the night and early morning was easier on the workers and guaranteed crisp, juicy fruit. Cheerful voices, in Spanish and English, ping-ponged back and forth across the parking area, greeting latecomers, sharing stories, and making small talk. The camaraderie and excitement were testament to the way people felt about harvest in Napa. Hard work went hand-in-hand with joyful thanksgiving for a bountiful crop. Even the tasting room crew was out in force, wearing work clothes rather than white shirts and slacks. Everyone wanted to be involved in the crush.

Margaret went in search of Davy. He had run off in the direction of the sheds earlier with his soccer ball in hand, his headlight blazing on his baseball cap, excited about getting up in the middle of the night. He'd begged to skip school for the day and help out, and she couldn't resist his eager anticipation at the idea of working alongside her at her new job. She caught a glimpse of his blonde head through the trees, where he was bouncing his soccer ball against one of the sheds with a Mexican boy a few years older than him.

"Davy, are you coming to work with me in the south field? We're getting ready to take off."

He caught the ball and turned around, then glanced back at his friend. "Want to come with us, Pablo?" he asked.

The boy shook his head. "I'm s'pose to stay by Uncle."

"Is Mario your uncle? I thought maybe he was your grandfather." Margaret put her arm around Davy and smiled at the boy. He looked about thirteen, with black hair and a scarred lip that pulled up slightly. He'd obviously been born with a cleft pallet and had gone through some reconstructive surgery.

He shifted nervously. "Uncle Mario's family is in Mexico—except for us," he mumbled, and then looked as though he wished he hadn't volunteered so much information. He stared down at the ground, scuffing the toe of his shoe in the dirt.

"If Mario wants you with him, that's fine," she said, changing the subject. She'd rather not know if

Mario's relatives were in the country illegally. The boy looked scared to death. She looked down at Davy. "Would you rather go with Mario and Pablo? I'll miss you, but as long as you promise to work hard…"

"Thanks, Mom!" Davy said, before she even finished her sentence, his voice pitched high with excitement. "We'll work hard, won't we Pablo?"

The other boy nodded solemnly.

"All right," she said, "I'll see you at breakfast."

The boys ran off to climb aboard Mario's truck, leaving her staring at Davy's deserted soccer ball and feeling much the same.

Ten minutes later Ernesto parked the truck at the far corner of the south field and let everyone off. Margaret and Billie climbed out of the cab and stood back while Ernesto directed the workers on different sides of the rows to begin picking. They each carried a small plastic bin that would hold about thirty pounds of ripe grapes, and their picking shears.

Billie worked on one side of a row, while Margaret took the other. The flashlights attached to their caps lit up the vines and revealed the plentiful clusters of purple grapes. The south field was planted in the seventies with Cabernet Franc and had always yielded the best crop of Fredrickson's varietals.

"Who is driving the tractor?" Margaret asked, hearing the put-put of the slow engine in the distance. The tractor pulled a long flatbed with huge bins attached. Each time the pickers filled the tractor bins, the driver would return to the winery to empty the load and the wine process would begin. The first step would be for the grapes to go through the de-stemmer/sorter machine.

Billie's light stayed pointing downward as she pinched off the grape clusters with her cutter and dropped them into the bin at her feet. She slid it along with one foot as she moved down the row. "Loren and Sammie are driving the tractors. I figured since they are two of the slowest pickers we have, but very careful in the tasting room with the crystal, that they would use extreme caution driving through the vineyard with our precious cargo."

"I hope they have more driving experience than just pushing a cart with glassware on it." She slid the bin along the row and clipped more bunches, dropping them into the quickly growing pile.

Billie laughed, her flashlight beam bobbing up and down. "Don't worry, they drove last year and managed to back the trailers in and out of the yard with awesome precision. I think Sammie actually pretends he's driving a big old semi. He told me his dream was to be a truck driver."

"He's still got time. He's another couple years away from retirement." Margaret heard the tractor getting close and lifted the bin. "Mine's already full. How bout yours?"

"Right behind you."

Half a dozen workers were already waiting to dump their bins by the time the tractor came to a stop behind the pickup. One of the men climbed up on the trailer and poured the grapes in the larger bins as each person lifted their container to him.

"How's it going Sammie?" Margaret called, when he shut off the tractor and climbed down to help.

"Pretty damn good," he said with a grin, as he always did when asked. He added, "Looks like these grapes were made for wine." An inside joke that had been around for so long no one knew who started it— or why it was considered a joke. But Sammie repeated it each harvest like clockwork.

"They sure do, Sammie." Billie's headlight flashed over his face and blinded him before she remembered to shut it off. "Sorry about that. It's actually pretty bright out here in the light of the moon. Forgot I was wearing it."

"We better get back out there." Margaret picked up her bin and headed for the place in the row that she'd marked with a white cloth on the ground.

Two hours later, Loren arrived with the other tractor, pulling another trailer bed of empty bins. They poured one thirty-pound bin after the other into the larger bins until the trailer was brimming with sweet/tart wine berries. He climbed back up to start the tractor and return to the winery.

"Loren, you mind if I hitch a ride back with you?" Margaret called. She handed up her bin and watched it get dumped into the gleaming pile. "I need to check on the sorting and start the press while they're still cool and crisp."

"I'll catch up with you later," Billie said. "Could you touch base with Adam—make sure everything's going all right? He's running the forklift and lifting the bins off the trailers." She laughed at Margaret's look of disbelief. "Don't worry. He shouldn't take anyone's head off. He has experience. He worked in a warehouse during college."

Margaret climbed up on the tractor beside Loren. "I'll check on him."

She held on as Loren put the tractor into gear and it jerked into motion, put-putting away down the gravel road toward the winery. The horizon was streaked with threads of pink, the first signs of daylight trying to break through. The winery was ablaze with light, the yard behind alive with motion. Adam had a bin on his forklift and was lifting it to the sorting machine as they approached. Another man watched the grapes fall in. Using a long fork he kept them from jamming up as they went through the machine and were de-stemmed and pushed along for sorting.

Loren pulled up close and shut off the tractor to wait his turn for the trailer to be unloaded. Margaret climbed down and stood looking around, loving the rhythm of harvest. The place was in full gear, everyone doing the job they'd been given. The thump and grind of the machines reminded her of Disneyland without music.

Loren hopped down beside her and adjusted the cap on his head. His hair was long and jet black like the feathers of a crow. He pushed it away from his face.

"How's it feel being chief today?" he asked. "A little nervous about making your first batch of firewater for the Fredrickson label?" Loren bragged that he was full-blood Karok Indian, but he sounded more like Hollywood's version of an Apache in a 1960's movie.

"I think I can handle it," she said. She yawned widely, suddenly feeling her lack of sleep. "I just need a large dose of caffeine in my bloodstream first. When Adam gets the trailer emptied, tell him I went inside to get coffee."

"Will do, Chief."

She started for the winery, but stopped and turned around. "Loren, when you were over at the other field, did you happen to see Davy and Pablo?" she asked.

He nodded. "Yep. They were there. At least the first time. I don't remember seeing Davy the last time I picked up, but he may have still been filling his bin."

"Thanks." She shook her head. "I know I shouldn't worry. There are a dozen people around." She didn't add that her father had freaked her out the other night with his nocturnal visit and she hadn't let Davy out of her sight since.

He raised his arm up to the sky and spread his fingers as though peering through them. "Morning sun race across sky. Boys run home filled with hunger." He sniffed the air. "Mmm, Sally cooking sausage links and French toast."

"You are quite the prognosticator."

"I was taught at my great-grandfather's campfire, many moons ago." He grinned and waved her off. "Go.

Have coffee with the squaws. Men will take care of things here."

Sally was busy in the tasting room ordering the caterers around. She saw Margaret come in and waved her over, still speaking to a young blonde woman with a huge metal serving dish in her hands. The woman finally moved past her and set it on the table in a heated compartment. Sally frowned and adjusted the temperature before moving toward her.

"I told them the crew probably wouldn't be in for another hour, but they want to get out of here. Apparently, they have another gig that pays a heck of a lot more than we do."

"Don't worry. I'm sure they'll be straggling in here a few at a time any minute now. I need caffeine."

Sally pointed to the beverage table. "Coffee, tea, or soda. Pick your poison."

Margaret filled a thermal paper cup with thick, black coffee and snapped a plastic lid on top. She took a careful sip of the steaming liquid. "I think that's dark enough to grow hair on Davy's soccer ball."

Sally laughed. "Want to make sure everybody stays alert."

"Hey, Loren's out there," she said, keeping her tone casual. Everybody knew they belonged together like salsa and chips, but neither would make the first move. "He's just getting ready to go back out to the field. Maybe you should ride along. Keep him company."

Sally actually turned pink at the suggestion, clashing with her red hair. "I don't have time for that. I've got to make sure everybody gets fed and the food stays hot," she said, moving back toward the serving tables.

"Really? Cause if I were you, I'd take a ride on Loren's tractor and watch the sun come up. You can't beat a romantic sunrise viewed from the seat of a tractor with a handsome Indian."

Sally glared at her. "What is going on?" she demanded. "Did he put you up to this?"

"Nope. This was all me. Everybody knows how you feel about him and how he feels about you. Isn't it about time you two got together and had a powwow?" She took her coffee and went back outside, leaving Sally standing motionless, unable to think of a thing to say for once in her life.

Adam caught Margaret's eye and strode toward her, a smile lighting his eyes. "There you are." He took the cup out of her hand and took a drink. "Ow, that's hot!"

"No kidding." She took it back and pulled the lid off so it could cool faster. "Has Sammie showed up with another load yet?"

He hooked a thumb over his shoulder. "He's back there now. I emptied his trailer already. He was talking to Mario."

"Mario's here?"

"Yeah, he drove up in the pickup. Said he was looking for Pablo. Apparently, the boys took off." He saw a shadow of fear climb her face like a storm cloud. "Don't worry. They probably just got bored and thought it would be cool to play tag in the dark or something."

She shook her head. "He promised me that he would work hard and stay put. He wouldn't run off without permission."

"Okay. We'll find him." He turned and saw Mario heading toward the sheds. He waved him over. "Mario! Over here."

The man hesitated, then turned and headed in their direction. A bright yellow bandana was tied around his head and he pulled it off to wipe at his face. "Miss Parker," he greeted, with a nod of his head.

"Mario, Adam said the boys are missing. How long has it been since anyone saw them?"

He rubbed at his neck. "Maybe…," he shrugged, "dos horas."

"Two hours? And no one looked for them?"

The man shook his head. "The men were working."

"All right," Adam interrupted. "Here's what we're going to do. Mario, go out and round everybody up for breakfast. Margaret and I will search the winery and the outbuildings. I'm sure they're either hiding in the vineyard somewhere to keep from getting punished, or they're off playing and don't realize what time it is." He put his arm around her and squeezed. "We'll find them."

Mario hesitated, whether unsure about following Adam's lead or confused by the language barrier, she wasn't sure. Finally he met her eyes. "Pablo's a good boy. No problema."

"It's not your fault, Mario. Go ahead and call everybody in for breakfast. The boys will show up. They're bound to be hungry," she said with more confidence than she felt.

***

Adam couldn't think of anywhere else to search. Every shed, outbuilding, cellar and barrel room, even Billie's house had been gone through. Mario had driven one of the pickups around the vineyard and called out their names over and over until his voice was hoarse. No one had noticed the boys since around three o'clock in the morning when they were seen working together to carry one heaped-to-overflowing bin to the trailer and had gone back down the row for the second. No one remembered if they returned.

"We were still on the backside of the Merlot then," said a chubby young man with a ring in his nose. "You don't suppose they would wander back to the canal? That thing can be treacherous. Kids drown in there every year."

Adam was glad Margaret had gone inside to call Handel, because he didn't want her hearing that, but as a mother, her thoughts had probably already gone in that direction. He turned around and saw her hurrying out of the winery with Billie following close behind. His sister caught his eye and waved him over.

"Thanks for your help, but there's nothing more you can do right now, so get back to the field and we'll let you know when we find the boys," Adam said to the men who had been pulled from their jobs to help in the search. "Billie needs everyone doing their job right now."

The men wandered back to the trucks, and prepared to return to the fields. He saw Sammie starting up the tractor and Loren moving toward his.

He hurried over where Billie now stood beside Margaret's car, leaning over the open door, speaking to her in a quiet voice. Margaret's face was ashen. She sat in the driver's seat and gripped the wheel so tight her knuckles had turned white. Billie stepped away when she saw him, and he leaned down beside Margaret, one hand on the roof of the car.

"Meg, where are you going?"

"Maybe he went home." She looked up, her eyes damp with unshed tears. "He used to hide in his closet and camp out. Maybe he's there."

"Let me go with you. I'll help you look."

"That's a good idea, Margaret. Take Adam with you," Billie said, placing her hand on his shoulder. "When Handel shows up here I'll let him know where you are."

Margaret shook her head, her gaze catching the winery returning to full motion in the rearview mirror. "No, you need Adam here. Everyone has a job to do. The winery can't just shut down because of two wayward boys. I'm sorry that I'm not living up to my job description today. But I don't want to pull anyone else away."

"I don't care about the wine," Billie said, meeting Margaret's eye. "I care about Davy and Pablo. Adam will go with you. The sooner you find the boys, the sooner everyone can get back to work."

She didn't argue. Adam straightened and kissed Billie on the cheek. "We'll find them," he said, and hurried around the car to climb in the other side.

Margaret put the car into gear and drove down the long gravel drive to the highway. An indigo blue sky stretched cloudless above them, the sun already warm enough to negate the need of a sweatshirt. Adam shrugged out of his and threw it into the backseat. He rested his hand on her shoulder, but didn't say anything until they pulled up before the Parker house. The shades were still drawn since they'd risen in the middle of the night. Margaret reached up to the visor to press the garage door remote.

"My remote's gone," she said, looking at him as though the world suddenly turned upside down and nothing made sense.

He looked around on the floor of the car and under the seats, then opened the glove box, but found nothing. "Okay, I guess you'll have to go in the front door."

"But where is my remote?"

He shrugged and climbed out of the car. "Why don't you check out the house and I'll look around outside. Is your shed locked?"

She shook her head. "No. It doesn't have a lock. Davy never goes in there. It's full of cobwebs and old equipment," she said, moving up the steps to the front door.

She selected the key on her keychain and stuck it in the lock. The door moved inward before she even turned the key. She jumped back as though she'd seen a ghost. "Adam…"

He hurried up the steps and moved past her to go in first, glancing down the hallway and into the living room, before inching his way toward the kitchen, his ears attuned to the slightest sound. The tennis shoes he wore made a slight scritching sound against the ceramic tile. He must have a piece of gravel lodged in a groove. The lights were still off in the house and with the drapes pulled the sun wasn't able to chase away the gloom. He neared the sliding door and heard the crunch of glass beneath his shoes before he noticed a jagged hole in the glass panel of the slider.

She was right behind him. "Someone broke my door!"

"This is where they got in. Must have gone out the front. Someone knew you would be gone to the winery and decided to do a little breaking and entering. You better check to see what's missing," he said, looking around for whatever was thrown through the window. He didn't find anything.

"The gun!" she suddenly yelled and went flying from the room.

He followed her to the kitchen and flipped on the light. She grabbed a chair, dragged it over to the refrigerator, stepped up on it, and reached over the decorative edge of the upper cupboards. She pulled the box closer and lifted it down. "Thank God, it's still here," she said, her face relaxing into a smile as she turned to face him.

"Glad to hear it."

She stepped off the chair and carried the box to the table. She lifted the lid and her face fell. "It's gone."

"What?" He looked inside. There was a jagged, fist-sized rock placed in the box where the gun once resided. "Well, we've found the break-in tool. Someone is playing games with us."

She met his gaze. "My father. He's the only one that would know about the hidden ledge above the cupboard."

"Would he take Davy as well?" he asked. The circumstances were too coincidental. The boys disappeared around the same time that Margaret's house was broken into and her gun stolen. What were the chances of that happening unless it was all part of some sick plan by Sean Parker to get even?

They both heard the sound of a car pull up outside and a door slam shut. A moment later Handel hurried through the open front door and into the kitchen, but stopped at sight of the box. "Why are you getting out the gun?" he said, looking from Margaret to Adam and back again. His face was tense, either from driving at break-neck speed to get home or at the knowledge that Davy was missing—probably both.

"It's gone. He took it," she said.

"Who took it?"

Adam felt a little awkward being in the room while they discussed their father, so he moved toward the garage. "I'll go check the shed and around the house for signs of the boys."

He didn't wait for an answer but went through the access door and pushed the button for the garage door to open. The door slowly lifted in a jerky fashion, the hinges groaning like they were in pain. Or was it the hinges? He turned around. The cellar door was propped open. Splintered wood lay scattered like matchsticks over the cement floor. He bent down and inspected the door. The wood was splintered and cracked along the edge. The padlock Margaret used to secure it was still attached to the latch, but the latch was no longer attached to the broken wood. It lay useless at his feet.

He peered down the stone steps and listened. There it was again. A low moan. Someone in pain. "Handel! Meg! Come quick!" he called, and stepped cautiously downward, pressing one hand against the wall as he descended.

They appeared at the top of the stairs behind him, silhouetted by daylight spilling through the garage door. "There's somebody down here," he said in a low voice. He moved slowly into the darkness, and still managed to trip on something. He caught his balance and reached down, grasped a long handle that was attached to a weighted head. A sledgehammer. It was heavy enough to smash a wooden door. He hoped it wasn't used for anything more.

He looked up. Handel was right behind him. He set the tool upright in the corner and searched for a light. Margaret called from the head of the stairs, "Is it Davy?"

Handel reached out and found the light switch. The barrels, machines, and table were as they were before. Margaret hurried down the steps, unable to wait any longer for an answer. Another moan. This time they knew it came from the direction of the wine storage cellar. Handel went in first.

"It's Pablo!" he called out seconds later.

They followed him through the narrow doorway. The boy was propped in the corner, beside the wine storage racks, his hands tied behind his back and a gag stuffed into his mouth, held in place with a piece of duct tape. His eyes were open, wild with terror. He flinched back when Handel bent over him.

"It's all right, Pablo. No one is going to hurt you. You're safe now." Handel gripped his arms and helped him struggle to his feet. "This might hurt though," he warned before he ripped off the tape.

The boy spit out the cloth, coughing and gulping air. "He took Davy!" he said finally when he caught his breath. "He said to tell you…" he stopped and gritted his teeth.

"It's okay, Pablo. Take it easy. Take a deep breath and start over." Handel spoke calmly, his hands on

Pablo's shoulders, making eye contact. "Now, what did he say?"

The boy gulped and his Adam's apple bobbed in his skinny throat. "I think he said, I mailed a letter to the birds in the old olive tree!"

Margaret bit her bottom lip and swayed like a reed in the wind. Adam caught her and wrapped his arms around her. He held her tight, stroking her hair. "We'll find him, Meg. We will."

Pablo's lower lip trembled as though he was about to cry, failure to remember the exact words weighing him down. Handel untied the boy's hands and patted his head. "You did great. It's all right."

Pablo looked around wildly then and pointed to the far corner of the cellar. "He gave Davy and me drugs. Something bad!" he said, clearly panicked by the memory. "I spit mine out!"

Adam looked behind the barrels and boxes. One half of a large tablet was wedged between two crates. He pushed them apart and picked it up. It was a huge pill, too large for any small boy to swallow hole. "Did you bite this in half?" he asked, worried that the boy might have harmful drugs in his system.

Pablo shook his head. "He gave part to Davy."

"We better get this to the police so they can send it to the lab. Find out what it is."

Silent tears coursed down Margaret's cheeks, and Handel appeared less than his usual confident self. He helped Pablo walk up the steps to the garage. The boy's legs were stiff and numb from sitting in the cold for so long.

Adam and Margaret slowly followed. He could see she was losing hope; the spark that drove her had been extinguished by the thought of her son drugged and possibly dying. He stopped and turned her around at the bottom of the steps. "Meg—look at me. We *will* find him. Don't stop believing."

She nodded, a small sob escaping before she straightened her shoulders and hurried up the steps.

***

Handel dealt with the police, as only a lawyer could, shielding Margaret as much as possible from the brunt of interrogation. They had all been questioned over and again. Why hadn't anyone seen or heard the boys being taken? Why were the boys here working instead of in school where they belonged? Why was Davy with the other crew instead of with his mother?

Anyone who had worked in a vineyard during harvest knew it wouldn't be hard to take the boys. Under the cover of darkness, with the noise of the tractor coming and going, workers calling and chatting back and forth, it would be quite simple. According to Pablo, Sean Parker threatened to kill Mario if they didn't go with him. He took their headlights and smashed them under his boot, then while the other men were at the trailer dumping their bins, he led the boys through the vineyard, staying to the shadows, until they crossed the road and headed toward the Parker house. Margaret's vineyard was last to be harvested and no one was at work there yet. He'd obviously stolen the garage remote from her car to set the stage for drama.

Margaret felt helpless. She didn't know what to do. The police had issued an Amber alert. They had a canine team scouring the fields. They told her to stay close in case her father called. Pablo never mentioned the olive tree when he spoke with the police. She didn't know if Handel had sworn him to silence or Sean Parker had threatened him earlier. She doubted it mattered. The police had less of a chance of understanding her father's gibberish than she did. She was more worried about the pill that had been found. They said they would call when they knew what Davy had been given. Maybe that would give them a clue as to where Sean Parker had taken him.

She sat in the kitchen staring blindly at the clock on the wall. She didn't know how long she'd been there until Billie drove up and walked in the front door unannounced. Handel and Adam had returned to the winery to aid the police in their questioning of the crew. But she sat alone waiting for a call that never came.

"Margaret, you've been sitting here in the dark for at least an hour. It's not doing anybody any good, especially Davy." Billie pulled up a chair and sat next to her. "The police will find him. You need to stay busy until they do. Handel said to forward the home number to your cell. That way you can come with me and you won't miss a call."

"All I can think about is how scared he must be. He's only nine." She shifted her eyes to Billie. "You know what that's like…being a small child in the clutches of a monster."

"You can't think like that," Billie said, her voice soft but firm. "Sean Parker is a monster, but he's also Davy's grandfather. I think in his twisted mind he actually cares about him. I don't believe he intends to hurt him."

She expelled a harsh sound, somewhere between laughter and tears, and shook her head. "No, he doesn't intend to hurt him, just drug and kidnap him, use him for extortion."

"Margaret." Billie leaned close and clasped Margaret's hand, forcing her to look up. "I know what it's like to be the victim and I know what it's like to wait for justice and closure. The only thing that kept me sane was staying busy."

Billie knew something about staying busy in a horrible situation. She'd dealt with so much and managed to come out the other side whole with just a few scars. Margaret knew Billie didn't like to talk about the past, to dwell on what she'd gone through, but she was a survivor and knew what she spoke of. So she got up, changed the phone, and followed her outside.

Billie dropped her off in the yard to supervise the crush and finally, in the business of working with the grapes, she found temporary solace. The pungently ripe smell of fruit mingled with the musky odor of Leo's sweat as he pushed the grapes into the de-stemmer with a long-handled fork. She lifted a cluster before it was pushed in. The skins were soft and not too dry—she bit one in half—the seeds nice and brown. They had picked at just the right time. Mario and Ernesto knew wine grapes even better than Jack Fredrickson or Charlie Simpson had. They were terrific vineyard managers. This crop would probably yield some of the best wine Fredrickson's had ever produced. Ironic really. On the worst day of her life, the best crop ever came in.

She sniffed and wiped at her eyes surreptitiously. Everyone was waiting for her to fall apart. But she wouldn't. Davy needed her to stay strong. He was proud that she was Fredrickson's new chief winemaker and she wouldn't let him down.

"Miss Parker." Mario stood at her elbow. He'd tied his yellow bandana around his neck now and wore a red baseball cap on his head. He pulled it off when she turned around.

"Yes?"

"Gracias. You find Pablo. My seester's son." He couldn't meet her eye but kept looking down at the ground as though ashamed that his nephew was found and her son still missing.

"I'm so sorry he got caught up in this. My father…Sean Parker is a monster." She couldn't go on. She drew a shaky breath. "I'm truly sorry. Take him home to his mother so she can hug him tight."

He nodded, but still hesitated. He had something more to say. "No se preocupe. El hombre malo va a pagar," he said. He slapped the cap back on his head and hurried to his pickup where Pablo sat inside waiting, his head leaning against the door, already fast asleep.

Margaret stared after him, her eyes narrowed against the noon sun. She had no idea what he said. Something about a bad man. Maybe. She watched him drive away and hoped Pablo didn't incur nightmares from his experience.

Leo climbed down from the machine with the fork in the crook of his arm. "That was weird," he said, with a shake of his head.

"What?"

"Mario." He inclined his head in the direction the pickup had disappeared. "He told you not to worry cause the evil man would pay."

"The evil man?"

"That's what he said. My grandfather speaks Spanish at home all the time. Believe me, I've heard the word *evil* more than once. He hates my music, my books, my girlfriends. To him everything's evil if it wasn't born or invented before 1950."

She and Leo had gone to the same schools, growing up. He dropped out about the same time she got pregnant, causing a lot of innuendo and gossip at the time. Leo had always been a player, but he had a soft heart and she could tell he was trying to lighten up the situation.

She smiled. "Thanks. I needed a laugh."

He shrugged. "No problemo."

Adam was bearing the next bin of grapes their way on his forklift. She pointed up to the top of the sorter. "Back to work, Leo."

***

"Where's my money?"

The gravelly voice set Agosto's teeth on edge. This man was a pox on society. He tried to hide his disgust. "You've managed to stir up the media. I thought we agreed to keep this off their radar."

Sean Parker laughed into the phone. "A secret kidnapping? There were a dozen people around and he happened to be hanging out with some other kid. Unless you wanted to turn it into murder, I couldn't very well keep it secret."

Agosto rolled his eyes at the stupidity of the man's statement. Since when did murder make things less worthy of media attention? He stared at the muted flatscreen on the wall of his hotel room. A picture of Davy and a prison photo of Sean Parker had been flashed on the screen at least forty times since he'd turned it on this morning. Parker would probably have a swat team on him before the end of the day. And Agosto couldn't afford to be in the country when it happened.

"Where is he?" He flicked off the television with the remote and strode to the window to look out at the city below. It wasn't nearly as calming as the view he'd had in San Francisco. And his nerves were already frayed from speaking with this imbecile. "We had an agreement. You wouldn't hurt him, just drug him so he doesn't remember anything."

"Did we?" The old man coughed, the phlemy wheezing sounded like he was on his deathbed. "I remember money being mentioned and I haven't received any. My grandson means a lot to me. A lot."

Agosto took a calming breath and released it. "You'll get your money when I get my son, but now I have to act the part of a distraught father. The whole production could take days. I wanted to be out of the country by tomorrow. I don't see that happening."

"Sorry. Sometimes kidnappings don't stick to the scrip."

Anger welled in him, but he kept his voice soft. "Take the boy to the place we agreed upon. I have someone to care for him. He will give you the money and you will disappear." He paused. "Mexico would be a good lifestyle for you. A nice hot, dry climate for your failing health, and lots of other kidnappers to sit around and swap stories with."

"I don't know what Maggie ever saw in you Salvatore, but you make me laugh," he said, dryly. "Don't cross me though, or you'll be laughing out the other side of your face."

CHAPTER ELEVEN

Adam spotted the blue convertible rolling up the gravel drive and cursed under his breath. Just what Margaret needed. He scanned the parking lot and saw that Handel's Porsche was still parked in the shade of the spreading oaks. He hurried inside the winery to look for him.

Sally sat at her desk, speaking to someone on the telephone. She lifted her gaze and covered the mouthpiece. "What?"

"Where's Handel?" he asked, obviously transmitting his need for speed, because she jerked her head in the direction of Billie's office. "He's with Billie."

"Thanks."

He strode down the hallway and didn't bother to knock, but thrust open the door to his sister's office. Handel sat on the edge of Billie's desk and she stood

168

beside him with her head on his shoulder and his arm around her. She pulled quickly away when Adam entered.

"Sorry," Adam said, "Handel, we've got a situation."

Handel's gaze narrowed and he stood up. "What is it? Is Margaret…"

"She's fine right now, but maybe not for long. I think you better come. That Salvatore guy just showed up."

"Damn!" Handel was out the front door before Adam and Billie. He strode down the walk and met Salvatore head on, his voice raised. "What are you doing here? You're not welcome!"

Salvatore stopped and looked at him as though he'd asked what color grass was. "I came as soon as I heard. What did you expect? My son has been kidnapped."

"He's your son when the situation calls for one. Carl told me how your father is pressuring you for an heir. It must be quite inconvenient to suddenly become a father when you've been living this terrific playboy lifestyle."

"How is Margaret doing?" Salvatore asked tightly, ignoring Handel's diatribe.

Adam glanced toward the yard where he'd just left Margaret going through a final inspection before sending a batch of grapes through the press. The Italian followed his gaze.

"I guess I'll ask her myself," he said and headed that way.

Handel grabbed his arm. "You're not going anywhere. This is private property."

"Handel! Stop it!" Billie stepped up and put her hand on his arm. "Let him go. He's Davy's father. He has a right to know what's going on."

"Stay out of this! You don't know what you're talking about."

His words cut Billie to the quick. She dropped her hand and stepped away. "Adam, go get Margaret," she said. When he hesitated she turned and locked eyes with him. "Get Margaret now. Neither one of you are helping by shielding her from reality. She needs to know what's going on. She's Davy's mother and he is Davy's father." She glared at each of them in turn. "Not you. And not you. Whether you like it or not."

Adam didn't have to fetch Margaret. She'd apparently heard the commotion and was already headed in their direction. A blue scarf held her hair away from her face and made her eyes appear large and luminous. Her mouth was set in a thin line, hiding the emotion fighting to get out.

Handel released his grip on Salvatore's arm and stepped back.

"Agosto," she said, holding out her hand. "I'm sorry I didn't call. You should have heard this from me."

He took her hand and held it briefly, his thumb caressing her skin. "It's quite all right. I understand. I imagine the police have kept you busy with questions."

"Yes, there have been a lot of questions and very few answers. My father…" she broke off and wiped at her eyes with the pads of her fingers. "I'm sorry. It's been a long day."

"I can only imagine. I wish I would have known sooner, so I could be here for you," he said, his voice dropping to an intimate, husky whisper. "Is there something I could do now?"

Adam wanted to toss him back in his fancy car and send him over a cliff but Margaret had a different idea. She took him to her office and closed the door. When they emerged thirty minutes later, her eyes were red from crying. She walked the man back out to his car, ignoring their hallway hovering and curious stares. Salvatore hugged her intimately, then got in his car and drove away. It was more than Adam could take. He strode down the hall, took the stairs two at a time to the cellar and waited to cool off.

***

The sun had long set and almost everyone had already gone home to get a few hours of sleep before they would rise to do it all again. The machines sat motionless, sleeping hulks of metal fading into the shadows of the yard. A neighbor's dog barked in the distance and then grew quiet as night settled down like an antsy child.

Margaret walked in the vineyard, down one row and up another, searching, hoping, enduring. The flashlight she carried lit up one side and then the other as she swung it back and forth in a rhythmic motion over the ground. Her eyes burned with strain, but she kept going, not knowing what else to do, unable to rest with Davy still missing. Maybe she could find something, a clue dropped by her bright son.

She heard a car start and glanced back toward the winery. Headlights cut a quick path toward her and then away as someone turned around and headed home. Probably Sally. She'd remained inside manning the phone in case word came about Davy. Even after Billie told her to go home, she stayed, adamant that they needed her.

"Margaret!" Handel called. "Wait up!"

She paused long enough for him to catch up—he was panting with the effort—then continued on. He matched her pace, not saying a word, and walked quickly along beside her as though they actually had somewhere to go.

"What are you doing?" he finally asked. "The police already had the dogs cover this whole area. You're not going to find anything. You should go home and get some rest."

"That's not going to happen," she said, swinging the light back to the left when she caught the glint of something shiny. She bent down closer. A foil gum wrapper. She straightened and continued on.

"Margaret," he pleaded, his hand on her arm, tugging for her to stop. "Please, don't do this."

"Do what? Search for Davy? I don't see anyone else doing it!" She jerked her arm away and glared at him in the dark.

"There's nothing anyone can do right now. We just have to wait."

"That's why I'm doing this," she whispered. "I don't know how to wait."

He fell into step with her again as she moved on. The cluster of old olive trees was just ahead, marking the end of the field. She flashed her light up into the branches for a second and then back at the ground, turning down the next row.

"Wait," Handel said, touching her arm.

"What?"

"The trees."

"So?" Even as she said the word a tiny spark of comprehension tore up her spine. She turned and pointed the light at the grove. "What's in the trees, Handel?" She should have known he'd understand the hidden meaning behind their father's message. His face had been too blank, his reaction too bland.

He took the flashlight from her hand and walked toward them until he stood right below the largest tree. Weathered and twisted by time and age, it stood sentinel over the vineyard. He shined the light up at the thickest branch and held it there. "See that?"

"I don't see anything." She cocked her head over his shoulder, gazing up into the dark branches, seeing only the face of the moon peeking through small crinkled leaves. "What am I looking for?"

"A birdhouse. The only thing he ever made with me. He was always in that woodworking shed of his, drinking, and doing God knows what else. I guess in spite of the way he treated me I wanted to please him. So I begged him to show me how to use the tools and make something. I built that little birdhouse. It wasn't much. He said I stunk at carpentry and should find another vocation." He dropped his arm to his side, and flicked the light off.

"Why did you put it clear out here?" she asked. A birdhouse was hung or placed where people could enjoy the activity, watch wild birds flit about looking for food and raising families.

"Because I was angry. He made fun of my work, so I told him I was going to smash it and throw it away. But I couldn't. Instead, I brought it out here and nailed it in this tree. A small refuge he couldn't take away. Or so I thought." He sighed. "I used to come here at night when everyone was asleep. This was my hiding place. I wrote letters and mailed them in the birdhouse."

"Who did you write them to?" she asked.

He shrugged. "I don't know. To God I guess. Spilled my guts on paper. Of course, he never wrote me back. But just putting the words down, acknowledging the way I felt—my anger, confusion—was a form of therapy. I managed to survive until he disappeared."

"So you never told anyone about this?" she asked, wondering why he was sharing it now. What did this boyhood refuge have to do with Davy's disappearance?

He didn't answer, busy testing the strength of a low hung branch. He dropped the flashlight, grabbed hold of the branch and swung himself up. Squatting low to avoid hitting his head, he braced his hand against the trunk and looked down. "I'll be right back," he said and started climbing upward.

It wasn't much of a climb for a grown man, but it did take him a few moments to maneuver between the tight branches, twisted with age. She watched him lose footing once and slide, nearly falling, but he caught hold of another branch in time. She bent down and picked up the flashlight he'd dropped in the process.

"You need some light?" she asked.

He must have reached the birdhouse. He was tugging on something. She pointed the light upward and caught his face in the beam for a second. His jaw was set with determination. "Not in my eyes!"

"Sorry." She moved the beam to the left and spotlighted the little wooden contraption he was yanking on. "Maybe you should just leave it there and take whatever's in it," she suggested. "It's been a long time. The tree has probably grown around it."

"I think you're right." He reached inside and pulled something out, stuffed it in his pocket without looking at it. He put his hand in again and felt around, but came up empty-handed this time. "That's strange."

He climbed back down and dropped to the ground. "My letters are gone. Not that they'd be in terrific shape, out in the weather for years, but I expected to find something left of them." He pulled from his pocket the one piece of paper he'd found and spread it open against the trunk of the tree.

Margaret peered over his shoulder, pointing the flashlight beam so they could both read it clearly. Printed in dark block letters on a piece of motel stationary, it read:

How does it feel to be the cause of so much pain? To know that you could have stopped all this if you'd just given me what I asked for? You're hurting your sister. You know that. You always wanted to cut corners and skip steps. Davy can come home when you follow directions and bring the items I requested. I'll be waiting. Don't let me down.

Your father, SP

Handel started to crumple it into a ball and then thought better of it. He smoothed it out and folded it carefully into fourths. "I'm sorry," he said, sticking it back in his pocket. "I should have given him the money. Maybe he would have gone away and left us alone."

"What are you talking about? He showed up the other night when you were with Billie. I didn't even tell you."

"He called me at the office. Demanded his share. Said that he heard about my engagement and knew I'd be coming into some money." He shook his head. "As if my marriage to Billie was about taking back the winery or something."

She flicked off the light and gazed up. The full moon was the color of butter tonight, a creamy orb against the night sky. Stars appeared one by one as her eyes adjusted. "Is it?" she asked, hating herself for the question, but needing to ask it. He'd always taken care of her and Davy. He knew she loved the winery and that she'd been extremely disappointed when Jack died and left it to Billie. The engagement seemed so sudden, without a hint of his intentions. Sure they'd been dating but…

"How can you even ask that? Did your relationship with Salvatore really scar you that much?" He took a step away, turned his back on her, and stared off into the vineyard for a moment.

"I'm sorry. It was a stupid question."

He slowly turned back around, hands pushed in his jeans pockets. "I love Billie. I intend to spend the rest of my life with her. That's what marriage is about. That's what *this* marriage is about. I don't care that she owns the winery, or even if she lost it tomorrow." He paused. "Sean Parker may have supplied half of our DNA, Margaret, but he's not our father. He is a crazy man with twisted perceptions. Don't buy into them."

"I wasn't," she said, but was relieved by his answer.

"Can we go home now? I can't leave you out here alone."

His cell phone rang before she could ask what other item besides money had their father requested.

"This is Handel Parker," he said, in his take-charge lawyer voice. "What? Where would he get something like that?"

"Who is it?" she asked, moving closer. "Is it the police? Did they find Davy?"

His expression changed from concern to anger, his mouth pulled tight at the corners. "I understand. No, I have no idea. Certainly. Thank you." He slipped the phone back in his pocket.

"Well?" She stared at his shadowed features, trying to read his thoughts. He rubbed a hand over his face and released a heavy sigh.

"The tablet was Ketamine."

She pressed her hands to her chest as though to protect her heart. "Tell me what that is."

"It's a powerful anesthetic used in horse surgery."

"What?" She barely breathed the word.

"Horse tranquilizer."

She closed her eyes and knew such intense self-recrimination that the pain was physical. Her stomach knotted and she bent over with a sob. Handel tried to pull her into his arms but she dropped to her knees in the dirt and screamed. There were no words, only wailing that bordered on hysteria. The wails continued and she couldn't seem to stop. Full-blown hysteria. The neighbor's dog began to bark, an empathetic howling.

Handel grabbed her by the shoulders and shook her. "Stop it, Margaret! This is not helping Davy! Get hold of yourself!"

"You knew! You knew all along he couldn't be trusted. But I felt guilty for not calling him when Davy went missing. I took him into my office and comforted him." She spit out the word, bitter on her tongue. "He said he prayed God would give him another chance to be a real father."

Handel bent down and lifted her by the elbows. This time she allowed him to pull her into the strength of his arms. When her sobs quieted, he pulled back. "Are you all right, now?" he asked.

She nodded, and wiped her face with the sleeve of her shirt. She'd never be all right until they found Davy, but it wasn't what he meant.

"The police already questioned him. He has a rock-solid alibi for his whereabouts at the time of Davy's disappearance."

"Of course he does. He would never get his own hands dirty. But we both know he's involved."

"Probably. It's too big of a coincidence for a horse tranquilizer to be the drug of choice. Although, the police did say that teens in rural areas have been found using it."

"They're not accusing the boys of taking it themselves?"

"No, they just asked if we knew of neighbors with horses. Somewhere the drug could have been stolen from."

"Did the police tell you what this drug does?" she asked, fearful of the answer but needing to know.

He nodded. "It produces euphoria and an inability to concentrate. Probably why they gave it to him. He wouldn't remember where he went or what happened and he wouldn't cause any trouble along the way."

"What aren't you telling me? I've seen drug commercials. Every drug has side-effects far worse than the problems they fix."

He hesitated. "It could possibly include numbness, vomiting or unconsciousness."

"Which means he could choke to death if no one is watching him," she said, panic gripping her insides again.

"Don't borrow trouble, Margaret. We have more than enough without worrying about *what ifs*."

***

Adam waited in the dark, leaning against an old piece of machinery. He watched the flashlight beam move through the vineyard, go off for a time, and then come back on pointing in his direction, like a giant firefly wandering aimlessly. The beam bobbed unsteadily and then went dark when Margaret screamed. The sound was gut-wrenching and he stood rooted to the spot, fearing the worst. He wanted to run into the vineyard, to be her shield against the pain, but Handel's voice carried across the field, "stop it Margaret!" and soon she quieted.

Billie had locked up the winery and retired to the house, still angry with Handel and him for the scene with Salvatore earlier. But she didn't know Salvatore, hadn't met him. She didn't know what a piece of work he was, that he shouldn't be trusted. Adam had a feeling the Italian playboy might have something to do with Margaret's emotional breakdown in the field. He gripped the edge of the smooth metal behind him and waited, digging the heels of his tennis shoes into the dirt.

Murmured voices reached his ears long before they left the field and crunched over the gravel drive toward Margaret's car. He moved out of the shadows and caught up to them as Handel opened the driver's side door and Margaret slid behind the wheel.

"Are you sure you don't want me to drive you?" Handel asked, even as his eyes strayed toward Billie's house.

"That's silly. You have your car here. I'll be fine." She pulled her seatbelt across and snapped it in place. "Besides," she said, "you need to talk to Billie. I don't know what you said to her, but she looked really hurt."

"I can go with her," Adam said, moving around the car. "I'll just walk back across the fields."

"That's not necessary," she said, turning the ignition. "I'm not a child."

Adam climbed in the car beside her, and smiled. "I'm not a child either."

"Good, you're both consenting adults to ride in a car. Glad to hear it." Handel closed the door and headed toward the house.

"I hope she lets him in," Adam said, glancing back. "Billie can be a tad stubborn."

"Must run in the family."

She was quiet until they pulled up outside her house. The garage was closed and she reached up to push the remote before she remembered that it was gone. She thrust the car door open and climbed out, her lips set into a thin angry line. "I hope they give him life for this," she murmured, digging in her sweatshirt pocket for the key to the front door.

Adam followed her up the steps and waited as she turned the key and released the deadbolt. He reached out and turned the knob and stood back for her to enter first. She hesitated as though afraid of what she'd find. He took her hand in his and they went in together.

She flipped the light switch beside the door and an overhead chandelier illumined the hallway and staircase that led to the upper level rooms. The kitchen was as they'd left it that morning after finding the broken window. The gun case was still on the table, open and conspicuously empty.

"Would you like some coffee?" she asked, her eyes darting about the room as though searching for a clue to the events of the day. She obviously wasn't interested in sleep or knew it would never come anyway. She opened a cupboard and pulled out a box of filters and a bag of ground coffee, then gave him a crooked smile. "I forgot," she said. "You don't really like coffee, do you?"

"I never said that."

"You didn't have to. I've never seen anyone nurse coffee so long without managing to taste it."

He shrugged. "I tasted it. I just prefer cocoa."

"You really are too young for me," she teased, filling the coffee pot with water. "Don't worry, I won't make you drink any."

"Thanks." He moved over to the broken slider. "You got a broom? I'll clean up this glass for you."

She pointed at the small closet door behind him.

He swept up the glass and put some duct tape over the hole in the window to keep the jagged edges from being a danger until it could be replaced. When he turned around she was sitting at the table with her head in her hands. Her shoulders shook as she cried silent tears.

He poured a cup of coffee and brought it to her at the table. She raised her head and tried to smile. A tear dripped off the end of her nose and she wiped her face with the tissue wadded in her hand. "You don't have to stay. Handel will be home later. You should go get some sleep. Billie will need you in the morning."

"Don't worry about me. I think I held some kind of record at college for the most consecutive nights without sleep." He held out his hand. "Come on. Why don't you lay on the couch and relax, and I'll play something for you."

She put her hand in his and he led her from the kitchen. The family room was more cluttered than usual and Margaret moved about picking up books and magazines and straightening pillows until Adam gently pushed her down on the couch, and swung her feet up before she could get back up.

"You came in here to relax, remember? Just lay there and close your eyes and you won't see the mess," he said. He picked up his guitar and slipped the strap over his head.

"But you will," she argued weakly, with eyes closed, a hand thrown over her face.

He breathed out a soft laugh. "I'm a guy. Messes are my life."

He began slowly strumming an old lullaby his mother taught him when he was a kid, soothing and mellow as a satin pillow, then moved on to something classical he'd learned in high school. He no longer remembered the name or the composer, but played from memory a version all his own. The composition always reminded him of water trickling over smooth stones in a mountain stream.

Her jaw grew slack in sleep, her lips parted slightly, and she pressed into the back of the couch. He watched her; afraid to stop playing for fear she'd wake. His fingers continued moving over the strings, as though they had a mind of their own. He played every slow, love song he knew and even managed to turn Rod Stewart's classic *Hot Legs* into a calming, slumber-inspired lullaby.

Finally, his fingers grew tired. She didn't wake when he stopped playing but curled tighter into the couch as though she were cold. He looked around the room and found a blanket folded over the top of the recliner. He carefully tucked it around her, feeling like he was in some chick flick and he was the rugged, romantic lead who falls for the beautiful, but tormented girl, who pretends to hate him, but is really head-over-heels.

He settled into the recliner and crossed his arms over his chest, watching her. He could only hope she felt that way about him. Her breathing turned heavy and her eyelids twitched as though she were dreaming. She moaned softly and curled her hands under her chin. He hadn't meant to come to California and fall for the first girl he met, but apparently he had. Now there was no going back.

The hairs on the back of his neck tingled and he turned his head to find Handel standing silently in the doorway. The man's shoulders sagged with the weight of responsibility. He stared at his sister, helplessness and fear deepening the lines in his face. Adam quietly stood up, revealing the fact that he was in the room, and Handel turned away, moving into the kitchen.

He followed.

Handel stood at the counter, his back to the room, pouring a cup of coffee. When he turned around he had regained his composure. He leaned against the counter and took a sip. "Thanks for bringing her home," he said, his voice barely above a whisper. "I didn't think she'd sleep. How'd you manage that?"

He lifted his hands. "Magic fingers."

Handel quirked his eyebrow but didn't ask. "Well, whatever you did, thanks."

"No problem." He rubbed a hand over his chin. "Can I ask what happened out there? In the vineyard?"

"Margaret didn't tell you?" He set his cup down and crossed his arms over his chest.

"I didn't ask her."

"Probably for the best. She didn't take it well."

That was obviously an understatement. Adam remembered the sound Margaret made, more like a wounded animal than a woman. He waited.

"The police called. Told us that the drug Davy was given was a horse tranquilizer."

"That's horrible."

"That's not the worst of it. Agosto Salvatore owns racehorses. He came to America to race one of them. He has access to such drugs. My father would not. But together they make a formidable team."

Adam shook his head. "Are you sure?"

Handel shrugged and picked up his cup. "I'm sure. Margaret's sure. The police? Who knows what they believe. They questioned him and checked out his alibi, but are they staking out his hotel to make sure he doesn't skip the country with my nephew? Doubtful."

"You know where he's staying?" Adam asked, reaching for the keys on the counter. Margaret wouldn't mind him borrowing her car for a few hours. Not for this.

"Sure. The biggest hotel with the fanciest..." he trailed off. "What do you have in mind?"

"I think someone should be watching him. Make sure he doesn't run off in the middle of the night."

Handel reached in his pocket and pulled out a money clip. He extracted three one hundred dollar bills. "It would be a lot easier if that someone were a guest of the hotel. They would have access to the underground parking as well."

He took the money and slipped it in his wallet. "I'll keep that in mind."

CHAPTER TWELVE

Adam drove slowly through the parking garage, searching for the blue convertible. There were so many fancy sports cars, he wondered if there was a mid-life crisis convention in town. After winding around up to the fourth level, he finally found what he was searching for. Blue metallic paint sparkled alluringly as he turned the corner and the headlights of his car flashed over the Ferrari. Salvatore had one of the best spaces available, wide enough for a huge SUV and far from any of those annoying concrete posts. His car had buffer zones large enough to keep any fellow drivers from parking too close and dinging his doors. Obviously he'd tipped the hotel's parking valet an exorbitant amount.

He found the nearest open spot and maneuvered Margaret's Toyota between the cement posts, hoping he could get back out without taking her side mirrors off. Another car drove past, tires squealing, not finding space, and continued to the next level. Very carefully, he opened his door and slid out between the tightly parked vehicles.

He walked nonchalantly toward the Ferrari, his gaze taking in the strategically placed security camera that covered this corner and pointed at the stairwell door beyond. He was tempted to lift the handle of the car as he passed, setting off the alarm, but he refrained. Bending down, hands on his thighs, he took a good look through the driver's side window. Agosto had left a cap on the passenger seat, the words *Golden Gate Racetrack* embroidered on the crown—a memento of his time here—other than that, the car was pristine, uncluttered.

Adam straightened and walked slowly around the vehicle to the stairwell. He took the stairs down to level two, then hopped on the escalator and rode it down to the lobby. The desk was attended by two men and an older woman, busy waiting on guests. The concierge sat at his own desk off to the side, speaking with a young couple while they tried to sooth a crying baby in a stroller. Adam stepped off the escalator and moved through the lobby toward the elevators. He'd already managed to find out what floor Agosto Salvatore was staying on. He pushed the up button and waited.

The chime sounded, heralding the elevator's arrival. The young couple caught up with him just as the doors opened. The man didn't appear any older than Adam, his dark hair cut short and spiked with some hair gel that smelled like citrus. He pushed the stroller, while his wife, her face scrunched in desperation, held a stuffed bunny over the baby's head in hopes of distracting it from continuing the ear-splitting screams emitting from tiny cherub lips. Adam wanted to cover his ears as he held the door for the family. He was sure the decibels emitting from the baby was more dangerous than the sound of a jackhammer.

"Sorry," murmured the woman as she passed him, shaking the bunny so close to the baby's face it was in danger of getting a mouthful of fur. She moved in beside her husband on the other side of the stroller and let her arm drop limply to her side. The baby continued to wail.

Adam tried to remain inconspicuous, pressing as close to the other side of the elevator as possible. He watched the numbers light up as they ascended and hoped the family would exit soon.

The doors finally opened on twelve and the man rolled the screaming child out the door. "We might as well go home tomorrow, Babe, cause pushing this thing around all day is not my idea of a vacation."

"Well, if your mother had been willing to watch him for one stinking week…" her voice dwindled away as the doors slid shut again.

Adam released a sigh of relief and leaned against the wall as the elevator slid up to floor fourteen and came to a stop. The doors slid open and he was face to face with a large black woman. Behind her, coming down the hall, was Agosto Salvatore. He quickly moved back into the corner of the elevator and pulled his cap low over his eyes. The woman looked at him strangely but stepped in and pushed the button for the lobby. He crossed his arms and stared down at the floor.

Agosto stepped in and turned to push the lobby button. Seeing it already lit up, he dropped his hand to his side and faced forward. The doors closed and the elevator descended. Staring at his wavy reflection in the brushed metal of the door, Agosto nervously combed fingers through his hair and straightened his suit coat. The elevator made stops at nine, seven, and four, and Agosto was pushed back as people entered, close enough that Adam could smell alcohol on his breath. When the doors finally opened to the lobby another group of passengers waited.

Adam, backed to the furthest corner in his attempt to be invisible, nearly missed his chance to get off the elevator. He pushed through oncoming traffic and stepped out just in time to see Agosto pause to chat with the concierge. The man smiled and gestured toward the front doors.

Salvatore moved toward the entrance, obviously expecting his Ferrari to be brought around any minute. He stopped and picked up a newspaper from a table, read the headlines, his mouth grim. He folded it and stuck it under his arm.

Adam took the escalator at a run, hoping Salvatore would be too engrossed in waiting for his car to look up. He nearly collided with an old man in Bermuda shorts and a straw hat when he opened the stairwell door. "Sorry," he said, moving quickly around him and darting up the stairs to garage level four.

He bolted through the door and ran to his car with the key fob out. Sliding between the vehicles, he squeezed back behind the wheel and started the ignition. The Ferrari was already gone from its space, but the valet had left orange cones to keep it saved from non-tipping customers. He threw the car into reverse and managed to inch out from between the pillars without scraping anything off. He turned toward the exit, his tires squealing like a litter of pigs. He couldn't lose Salvatore now. He prayed all the lights turned red so he could catch up. Better yet, that the smug rich boy would get picked up for drinking and driving. That would put him out of commission for a while.

Pulling up to the parking attendant's booth, he saw a flash of blue move under streetlights and turn, disappearing from his view. He signed the card and handed it back, stepped on the gas as the bar was raised.

By the time he hit the street, the Ferrari was pulling away from the front of the hotel, the valet waving him off. He slowed, waiting for Salvatore to pull into traffic, then followed, keeping two or three cars between them for a buffer.

Once the city lights faded behind them, Salvatore sped up, his car weaving in and out of traffic as if he were driving in the Indy 500. Adam struggled to keep close enough not to lose him without getting himself killed in a head-on collision.

He opened the vents and let the cool night air in, heavy with the sweet scent of sun-ripened grapes. He glanced at the clock in the dash. Half past nine. If Salvatore was driving back to San Francisco tonight, he hadn't brought his luggage. But maybe that was a ploy to throw anyone watching off his tail. The police may have asked the hotel to let them know when he checked out.

Wherever he was going, he was in a hurry to get there. Adam kept his eye on the taillights. Traffic thinned as they drove further out and he pulled back, not wanting to spook him. He'd watched enough cop shows to know the bad guy was always paranoid. Apparently for good reason.

He suddenly realized they were nearing the winery. He saw the sign for Fredrickson's lit up by the Ferrari's headlights as it sped past, and he followed slower, glancing toward the house. Hunkered down in the shadow of the giant oaks, it seemed much smaller than it actually was. Billie still left a light on in the hallway at night, but all looked dark from his vantage point. He hoped she was getting some sleep, but she was probably sitting up wondering why he hadn't come home and worrying about Davy. He should have called.

The Ferrari's brake lights came on and the car pulled quickly over to the side of the road just past the Parker driveway. Adam continued on, hoping Salvatore hadn't spotted him. He looked in his rearview mirror and saw the Ferrari make a u-turn and speed back the way they came. He cut his lights and pulled to the side of the road, waiting to see what Salvatore was up to.

A truck barreled past, shaking the little Toyota, and him to the core. This was a dangerous piece of road and here he was sitting alongside it in the dark. A few seconds later the Ferrari's brake lights glowed red once again and the car turned off the road. Salvatore either pulled into the winery or the little dirt-packed access road that wound down between Fredrickson's vineyards and the neighbor's fields on the other side.

Adam flicked his lights back on, waited for two cars to pass, and then whipped the Toyota back around onto the highway. He slowed when he neared the Fredrickson sign, but no car was in sight. He cut his lights and turned into the winery driveway. He thought he caught a glimpse of movement in the field to his right, but if Salvatore had actually driven his precious sports car down that rutted road, he was also playing with lights out. The road was only meant for workers on tractors or other machinery; a rough piece of dirt track that would destroy the shocks on something so low to the ground. Salvatore would probably have to abandon the car before he went far.

Adam parked the Toyota near the winery and stepped out, closing the door softly. He stood and listened, hoping to catch the sound of the performance engine whimpering in agony, but the night was quiet around him. He took to the shadows, staying close to the buildings and trees, making his way back toward the access road. He thought he heard someone cough and paused to listen. The neighbor's dog barked across the field, probably chasing a rabbit. He moved on, pulling back vines and crawling under a row of grapes, then another. The access road was hard-packed and rutted. He followed it toward the highway keeping to the shadow of the vines. The moon, obscured by a swath of cloud cover for the moment, gave him much needed invisibility, but he knew it wouldn't last for long. Clear skies were obviously the curse of California. At least for someone wanting to move about in the dark undetected.

The Ferrari, as he suspected, had been deserted close to the highway. The wheelbase would never survive this terrain. Salvatore was gone, a faint scent of cigarette smoke lingering in his wake. Adam turned and moved back the way he'd come. Why would the man be out here at the winery in the dark? Was he planning on walking all the way around to Margaret's place, or was he up to something else?

Nearing the winery, he thought he heard a voice on the wind, a murmur that rose and faded away, followed by a short, harsh laugh. He paused, wondering whom Salvatore was meeting. The moon slid out from behind clouds and lit up the yard like a theatre spotlight for just a moment. Adam slunk back against the wall of the shed and inched forward to peer around the edge. He didn't see anyone. Wherever they were standing was out of his line of sight, and he was afraid to venture further and be seen. Another voice—murmured words indecipherable at this distance, but the feeling behind them was clear.

Anger.

The moon disappeared again, and he moved back around the building in the other direction, hoping to come up behind them and hear what they were saying. Somewhere in the distance a radio was suddenly turned up, the happy stuttering trumpets of a Mariachi band. The neighbors were probably working through the night to bring in their harvest.

He rounded the building fairly quickly, moving toward the work yard. The black hulking shapes of a tractor and trailer lay before him, his familiar forklift—an eerie specter—crouched beside the sorter. Somewhere close a car backfired and he automatically ducked. His pulse accelerated as he stood there listening hard to decipher meaning out of the silent aftermath. Realization flooded his mind. Not a car backfiring, but a gunshot. The sound had been close, echoing off the walls of the winery.

Leaning back, he pulled his cell phone from his pocket. Who should he call? The police? Handel? He flipped it open and the face lit up. Flipped it closed again. What if this person with a gun saw the light? He crouched low, listening. The porch light came on at the house, lighting a path halfway across the gravel. He heard the squeak of the screen door as Billie looked out, her dark hair shining in the overhead bulb. She glanced around, then closed the door and shut off the light.

Adam released the breath he'd been holding and slowly stood up, stretching the kink in his back. Everything was quiet again. No voices. No nothing. Maybe it wasn't a gun he'd heard. Maybe it really was a vehicle backfiring in the neighbor's fields—or something else. The bang could have come from a machine.

Staying to the shadows, he moved forward. Someone grunted, struggling with something heavy behind the machinery, a scooting sound and a thud accompanied by heavy breathing. He waited what seemed like an interminable amount of time. Just when he'd decided to confront the person, he heard the Ferrari start. The soft purr of the performance engine was unmistakable even at this distance. He turned and raced back around the building and down the dirt track, hoping he didn't trip in a rut and twist his ankle. The car's headlights sliced on, blinding him. Thrust into reverse, it moved backwards at a dangerously damaging speed, bumped back onto the shoulder of the highway and spun around in the gravel, gears grinding. Adam watched as the car spun out in the gravel and shot forward like a bullet, rubber squealing as it found purchase on solid blacktop, and headed back toward town. Red taillights winked and slowly disappeared into the night.

He coughed and covered his nose against the assailing blanket of dust. Salvatore had tricked him. He must have known he was being followed. Was one of Billie's employees also in on the kidnapping? He turned and ran back toward the winery. By now, the other person would have had sufficient time to disappear.

He didn't hesitate this time, hoping to catch the culprit before they got away. No doubt the pounding of his shoes against hard-packed earth was as loud as a battle cry. He ran toward the machines, silent in slumber, hoping to surprise his opponent, but nothing moved. The only sound was the distant Mariachi band playing another happy harvest song on the radio. He picked up a metal fork leaning against the sorter and raised it over his head like he was going spear fishing.

"What are you doing out here?" A voice demanded. A flashlight flicked on, blinding him. He whirled around brandishing the fork. Billie jumped back and gasped. "What the…!"

"Billie!" He dropped the fork and stood there in the beam of the flashlight, blinded and dumb.

"Adam? I heard something and thought someone was breaking into the winery. I called the cops. They'll be here any minute." She shook her head. "Now what am I going to tell them? That my stupid brother was roaming around in the dark, and nearly assaulted me with a sorter fork?"

"Could you point that thing down a bit? You're killing me here," he said, holding a hand over his eyes.

She lowered the beam to the ground. "What *are* you doing out here?"

"Could I see that flashlight please?" he held out a hand and she reluctantly handed it over.

"Well?"

He moved around the sorter, shining the light over the ground, looking for something to prove that someone other than himself had been skulking around the winery. He bent down, squinting at the dirt. What looked like tracks from a bobsled being pulled across the ground, equally spaced marks, led past the sorter and along the belt that carried the grapes into the winery to be pressed. The marks stopped at the edge of the concrete walkway that rounded the building. There was nothing around that would make those dragging marks. One of the large grape bins, pushed against the wall, filled with the cast off fruit and stems that went through the sorter and was rejected, was the only thing within ten yards of the marks.

He straightened and blew out a frustrated breath. "Salvatore was meeting someone here. I don't know what they were up to, but they took off."

"Was it Sean Parker?" she asked, clearly repelled at the thought that the man could have been right outside her door.

"I don't know. Never saw him. I was actually wondering if Salvatore had an accomplice here at the winery. Someone who could help Parker get the boys away without anyone being the wiser." A siren whined in the distance. "The cavalry's coming to save the day."

She took the flashlight from his hand. "None of my employees would be involved in Davy's kidnapping," she stated emphatically. "Don't even go there."

He held up his hands. "Sorry. Just thinking out loud."

"Well think silently," she said. The police turned up the driveway, sirens silenced now, but lights still flashing. She moved to meet them, then stopped and poked Adam in the chest. "Has this got something to do with Handel?"

"I left Handel at home with Margaret. I saw Salvatore pulling into the dirt road behind the winery with his lights off. So I followed him." He left out the part about the hotel but he figured it wouldn't help his case with the police.

Red and blue lights flashed, reflecting on the front of the house like a child's mobile. "Let me do the talking," she said, hurrying toward the cruiser.

***

Officer Stanton pulled his cruiser closer to the yard, headlights on bright and a side-mounted spotlight flooding the yard with enough light to grow marijuana. He and the other officer, were both holding flashlights big enough to do double service as billy clubs, roamed the yard, searching behind the machinery and around the sheds.

Adam pointed out the tracks and Officer Stanton shook his head. "Could be anything. Are you sure you didn't see anyone?"

"It was too dark, and I wasn't close enough to hear what they were saying."

"But you heard a gunshot?"

"It sounded like a gunshot." He shrugged. "But I don't know. It echoed between the buildings strangely. Could have been a vehicle backfiring in the field I guess."

"But you did see Mr. Salvatore's car?" The officer asked, his brows raised.

"Yes sir. A convertible Ferrari is hard to mistake even in the dark. I thought it was strange when he pulled into the access road. It's dirt and very rough. Not a great surface for a sports car."

"Okay, we'll check it out." He turned toward Billie. "Ma'am, let us know in the morning if anything seems out of place or missing."

"Are you sure you don't want me to go inside and turn the outside lights on?" she asked, pushing her hair behind her ear.

"If anyone was still hiding here we would have found them." He met Adam's eye and jerked his head toward the Toyota. "Is there some reason Margaret Parker's car is over there?"

"I borrowed it," he said, hoping they didn't call Margaret and check out his story. They'd obviously run her plates.

"Okay." He tipped his hat. "Good night, folks. We'll have a patrol car come up your road a couple times tonight. Keep an eye on the place."

"Thank you, officer." Billie grabbed Adam by the arm and pulled him toward the house. "You've got a lot of explaining to do.

CHAPTER THIRTEEN

Margaret woke to the smell of frying bacon. She licked her lips and pulled the blanket closer under her chin, refusing to open her eyes. Handel and Davy were trying to tempt her from her bed on a Saturday morning again, so they could talk her into doing something she wouldn't want to do. Like visiting the San Francisco Zoo or going fishing—two things she could live without ever doing again. She tried to roll over on her side and felt the back of the couch against her face. Her eyes shot open.

Davy! She pushed the blanket back and sat up, looking wildly about the room. Had it all been a dream? If so, why was she sleeping in the family room? She stood up too quickly and dark spots clouded her vision. She sat back down and dropped her head in her hands.

"You're up," Handel said from the doorway. "I made breakfast."

She met his somber gaze. "Davy?" she asked.

He shook his head. "No word yet."

Tears came unbidden, welling in her eyes. She blinked them away. She moved from the couch to the kitchen, went through the motions of life, ate because Handel expected her to, spoke when spoken to, but inside she felt dead, like life had been sucked out of her body.

"Did you hear me?" Handel asked, setting his coffee cup down.

She stared at him, completely blank. "Sorry?"

"Adam called."

"About what?" She gathered the dirty plates and forks and carried them to the sink.

"There was an incident at the winery last night. He'll tell us about it when we get there." He stood up and pushed his chair in. Glanced at his watch. "How soon will you be ready to go? It's almost three."

"Why are you even up?" she asked, the fog in her brain clearing enough to realize something wasn't right. "I can drive myself to the winery. You never get up before five. What's going on?"

"You don't remember? Adam was here last night. He drove your car back to the winery." He refilled his coffee cup and sat back down to read the news on his laptop while she showered and dressed.

She remembered Adam coming home with her the night before. Insisting that she lay on the couch and rest while he played his guitar. He could probably sooth a beaver with a toothache by playing that thing. She remembered closing her eyes against the flood of pain that thoughts of Davy brought. She tried to shut out the fear that grasped her heart with fingers so tight she could feel it clear to her toes. The music had washed over her like a spring of hope, withering fear. At least temporarily.

She pulled a t-shirt, hooded sweatshirt, and jeans on, pushed her feet into sneakers and went into the bathroom to brush her teeth. Her reflection in the mirror reminded her of her mother, toward the end when all hope was gone for recovery, the light that once glowed from her skin, her eyes, her very soul, was dim and yellowed, like a bulb before the element snaps and goes out forever. Could an emotional death be as permanent as a physical one? If Davy wasn't found, if something terrible happened to him, how would she survive it?

"Margaret?" Handel called up the stairs. "Are you about ready?"

She brushed her hair back and pulled it into a ponytail. Closing her eyes, she prayed to go back in time—that this day would end the way the day before began—with Davy beside her.

At the bottom of the stairs Handel waited, his lips curved up into the semblance of a smile, but his heart was definitely not in it. She moved past him, giving his hand a quick squeeze. "You don't have to pretend for me."

He followed her out the door and locked it behind him. "I should warn you that reporters may show up at the winery today. They can't legally camp out here because it's private property, but the winery is a business. Billie is trying to get the police to keep them away since Fredrickson's is supposed to be closed during harvest. Not that a closed sign will deter the wolves from a story."

It was inky black outside, the kind of dark that slowly deepens through the night until it feels as though you could touch it. The moon was hiding when they pulled up outside the winery, but the yard was already bustling with people in motion. Handel parked the car close to the house and they got out.

Billie was watching for them. She opened the front door and waved them in. "I'm glad you're here." She let Handel pull her into an embrace, but stepped out of his arms rather quickly as though she wasn't quite finished being mad at him. "We have a lot to discuss."

They settled in the living room, Adam hovering protectively over Margaret's shoulder where she sat in an overstuffed chair, while Billie and Handel took opposite ends of the couch. Through the open window they could hear machinery start up, voices raised as the crew resumed work, and the sound of the tractor returning to the field for another load of grapes.

"When Adam followed Salvatore last night," Billie began, "he ended up back here at the winery." She put up a hand to stay questions. "He was meeting someone."

"I couldn't see them. They were behind the machinery or something. It was really dark," Adam said, in his defense.

"And why were you following Agosto?"

Handel and Adam locked eyes and looked quickly away.

Billie shook her head, looking annoyed with them both. "They thought he might lead them to Davy. But he just came back here. We haven't figured out why. The police looked around but whoever was here had already gone, and nothing seemed out of place."

"Are you positive it was Agosto?" Margaret asked.

Adam hunkered down beside her chair so he could look her in the eye. "I followed his Ferrari from the hotel. There's no denying he's involved in this somehow."

"Isn't it possible my father was trying to extort money from him because he knows he's wealthy, and Agosto met with him to make an exchange for Davy?" She sounded desperate to exonerate the father of her son, and after all he'd put her through she didn't know why she cared, but it felt wrong to blame him without proof.

"At this point, anything is possible," Billie said, and looked away.

"I wouldn't hinge my hopes on that bastard being the good guy." Adam moved to stand at the window, his voice harsh. "He took off like a bat out of hell.

Probably did some damage to the undercarriage of his car the way he was driving over those ruts. He did not want to be found out. Other than in movies, heroes rarely dress in tights and masks and hide their identity in the dark. Most times that practice is reserved for crooks."

"Adam," his sister warned.

"No. He's right." Margaret got up and moved behind him. Adam's shoulders were stiff, his arms crossed tightly over his chest. She put her arms around his waist and leaned into him, her chin resting on his shoulder. It felt right. He relaxed. "You are all trying to protect my feelings, when what we really need to do is find Davy." She reluctantly released her hold on Adam and turned around. "What cock and bull story did Agosto give the police for last night?" she asked.

"Haven't heard," Billie said. She glanced toward Handel. "They said they'd let us know."

Handel reached out to clasp her hand. A silent apology. He stood up, slowly releasing her fingers. "I'll call and nag them until they do. I'm going to drop by Carl's place and see if he's been in touch with his cousin. Then I'm going to use the media to harass Agosto Salvatore until he cracks. If anyone can do it, channel five news can. They always get the story first," he quipped, his tone as dry as shoe leather.

At the car he kissed Billie goodbye. Adam and Margaret looked on from the front steps. When he pulled back, his gaze strayed over her shoulder toward his sister. "I'll tear the Golden Gate Racetrack apart stone by stone if I have to Billie, until we find where they've hidden Davy. That man will not take my nephew out of this country."

***

Margaret was on the press floor when the first news van pulled up. She watched the grapes topple from the bin into the giant rolling press. Adam backed the forklift away and got off to watch. Leo had climbed up on the press and was packing the grapes with his hands. It was still the best way although he'd probably be stained for days. Once the press did the work, they would drain the free run juice.

"Ms. Parker, I'm Jane Goodall with channel five news. Could you tell us what you know about the disappearance of your son? Why did your father take him and did he leave a ransom note?" The familiar looking blonde woman thrust a microphone in her face. She wore a tight skirt and three-inch heels, and enough makeup to bake a cake.

Margaret backed away, clamping her mouth tight.

The reporter moved closer, carefully stepping around a pile of smashed grapes. "Have you spoken with the boy's father, Agosto Salvatore? My source says that you have a restraining order against him. Has he been abusive to you or your son? Do you have any reason to believe he is involved in your son's kidnapping?"

"Get out. You have no right to be here. We are trying to work and you are in the way," she managed to say without slapping the woman.

"Ms. Parker, I'm sorry we've interrupted your work, but I know you want to find your little boy and the best way to get the word out is through the media. If you'd be willing to be interviewed, I can guarantee that millions of people will be watching. And that is a lot of eyes looking for your son."

"She said to go," Adam said, placing a hand over the microphone.

Jane Goodall turned toward Adam, and smiled her slick reporter smile. "And who might you be? The boyfriend? The handyman?" She raised her brows. "I bet you are very handy."

"Ms. Goodall, may I speak with you in private?" Margaret gestured toward the door that led into the distilling room.

The woman waved her cameraman away and followed her through the door.

With the door shut, Margaret leaned against it. She released a breath. "I saw your interview with Agosto, Ms. Goodall, and I know you slept with him."

The reporter gasped and started to protest.

She held up a hand. "No point in arguing. Let's come to an agreement. I won't bring up your sordid affair with a man the police have under investigation, and you won't harass my friends or myself. I'll give you an exclusive interview this afternoon if my son has not been found."

Her lips curved up into a slow smile. "What about if he is found?"

"Either way then."

She held out her hand. "You have a deal."

"Good. I'll call you."

"No need for that. We'll be here waiting."

Margaret moved away from the door and Jane Goodall reached for the knob. "By the way, how old are you?" she asked. "You look much too young to have a nine-year-old son. Agosto Salvatore doesn't happen to have outstanding statutory rape charges against him as well, does he?"

"You'll have to save that question for later."

She nodded. "I look forward to it. I hope he does have something to do with this. Between you and me and the door, I'd love to nail that bastard's hide to the wall."

"Get in line."

***

Officer Tate and his partner showed up at 9:00 am and were ushered into the conference room by Sally. The reporters had tried to push their way into the winery, but Sally was a bulldog when it came to protecting those she cared about. She set Loren to guard the front door and called in Billie, Margaret and Adam to hear the latest. The officers refused to sit but stood just inside the door of the conference room, their expressions grim. Margaret stood also, arms pressed tight around her middle.

"I called Handel. He was just getting out of a meeting. He'll be here as soon as he can," Sally said, and excused herself from the room.

Billie moved beside Margaret and put an arm around her for support.

Adam stood with his hands braced on the back of a chair.

"After the incident last night here at the winery, we went to the hotel to question Mr. Salvatore," Officer Tate began. "The front desk couldn't get him to pick up the phone in his room. But the concierge said that he always uses valet parking, so we questioned the men on duty. They were positive he had not returned. Apparently, he's a big tipper."

"I saw him head back toward town," Adam said, "but he could have turned around and drove straight to San Francisco in a couple of hours. Do you have an APB out on him?"

"What if he has Davy with him? What if he takes him on his private plane and leaves the country?" Margaret's voice rose shrilly.

The other officer shook his head, his voice a mellow rumble. "Ma'am, please calm down. We have an APB out on Agosto Salvatore and Sean Parker. We'll find them."

"The thing is," Officer Tate said, glancing at his partner, "Salvatore's rented Ferrari was found deserted in the ditch just west of here along a gravel road that doesn't get much traffic. A passerby called it in this morning once it was light out. A forensics team is going over it now."

"What does that mean?" Margaret asked.

"It means he had an accomplice pick him up or he hitchhiked. Either way, he's on the run. We'll find him, Ma'am." Apparently he'd decided that Davy's father wasn't such an innocent man, only wanting visitation rights and a chance to get to know his son. He continued. "He didn't check out, so we are waiting for a search warrant to go through his suite and whatever he left behind. Hopefully, since he wasn't intending to leave quite yet, he left a clue to his next move."

"I know what his next move is—to take my son out of the country! You have to stop him."

"Ma'am, we're doing all we can." He glanced toward Adam. "From what you told us about last night, it sounds as though Mr. Salvatore doesn't yet have possession of his son—that he was meeting Sean Parker to make an exchange. Which means, if he does manage to leave the country, it will most likely be without Davy." He held Margaret's teary gaze. "I think we need to focus more on your father, Miss Parker. He knows this area well, and where he might hide a young child."

Margaret felt Billie tense up beside her. The conversation had to bring up horrible memories of one summer of her childhood that she'd rather forget. She reached down and clasped the hand of her friend. "He does. In fact he left a note for Handel last night in the olive grove at the end of the vineyard."

"Why wasn't this reported immediately? I just spoke with your brother early this morning."

Billie and Adam looked surprised as well.

"I don't know. So much has happened, Handel must have forgotten to mention it." She bit her bottom lip and hoped he arrived soon.

"What did the note say?" Officer Tate asked, pulling out his little notebook.

"It said Davy would be returned when Handel gave my father what he wanted."

"Money?"

"He called Handel days ago and asked for ten thousand dollars. Before Davy disappeared."

"The note wasn't specific?" He glanced up, his pen still against the page.

"It was written for Handel. He didn't explain it."

When Handel finally got there, they were all waiting a bit impatiently. "Officers," he greeted, glancing around the room. "Did I miss something?"

"I told them about the note."

"The note?"

"The ransom note you neglected to mention," the big officer explained, a suspicious frown forming between his brows. "Didn't you think that was an important piece of information in finding your nephew?"

Handel cleared his throat. "I think we all know that my father is doing this for money. He asked both of us," he gestured toward Margaret, "for money this past week. When we turned him down he went to Salvatore. Salvatore already had an agenda, so he took the bait. The note my father left for me was more of a kick in the ribs than any real ransom note. He wants me to know that he's still in control."

"Mr. Parker, we're in control. I need that note," Officer Tate said firmly.

"I'll get it for you. It's in my car."

***

When the officers had finished grilling Handel, they left, with a promise to report back if Salvatore was picked up or if any leads cropped up from the search of his suite.

Handel took Margaret aside into the tasting room. The tables were empty, no white cloths or crystal. Everything had been put away until harvest was through. It seemed bare and lonely, the black and white photographs hanging along one wall, a simple reminder of how time changed everything. "Why did you bring up the note?" he asked.

"Why wouldn't I? Davy has been kidnapped. The police need to have all the pieces to solve the puzzle. Don't you think that's important?" She glared at him. "What are you trying to hide? You still didn't explain the note. I have a right to know! What other items did he want you to bring besides money? And why are you trying so hard to make it seem inconsequential?" She didn't bother to lower her voice and knew that Adam and Billie could probably hear them in the other room.

Handel expelled loudly. "Why can't you trust me? I'm not Salvatore. I'm your brother. I've watched out for you and Davy all these years. Do you think I'm plotting against you now?"

"I just want him back," she whispered, tears pooling in her eyes. "Can't you see I'm broken? Trust has nothing to do with this. It's about finding Davy, and you aren't helping by hiding information."

"I'm sorry." He rubbed a hand over his face in that slow way he had when he was thinking. "I should have told you."

"Told me *what*?"

He glanced toward the doorway. "He wanted the pictures."

"Pictures?"

"The pictures of his victims. The Polaroids that Billie has. Pictures of the children he molested," he said, his voice sharp with disgust. "He said they belong to him. And I don't think he meant the photos—but the girls. Like he owned their souls. I couldn't do that to Billie."

The thought of what her father was capable of made her nauseous. She focused on breathing until the feeling passed. She asked, "How can she still be in possession of the pictures? I thought you handed them over to the police when he was arrested last time."

"No. Sam Harper was the only officer that knew she had them. When he died last year, that information went with him. Billie didn't think it was fair to the other girls to hand over their photos without asking them first. She's been trying to contact each one as she finds out who they are. Unless they've been repressing their memories as well, the statute of limitations is up for them to bring a case to court anyway." He sighed.

"Billie's testimony put him back behind bars. She thought it was enough to keep him there."

"It should have been enough to keep him there," Billie said, stepping through the doorway. She'd obviously been listening, her lips pressed in a hard line. "Your father has caused only pain his entire life. Isn't it about time we put a stop to it?"

He looked away. "What can we do, short of killing him?"

Margaret saw weariness around her brother's eyes and mouth that weren't there before, even when he worked outrageous hours during important court cases. She realized he hurt as much as she did. He was just better at holding it in, trying to be strong for both of them, but the shell was beginning to crack.

"We can give him the pictures in exchange for Davy, and let the police arrest him." Billie's hands were clenched into fists at her sides. "Those girls would not want another child to suffer if there was something they could do about it. Believe me, I know."

"I know you do, Billie. Thank you." Margaret went and hugged her tight. Billie remained stoic and stiff, before finally melting into her embrace, a lone tear sliding down her cheek and onto Margaret's shoulder. Margaret looked up and found Adam watching from the doorway, his eyes resting on her warmly.

"That's all well and good, if the police don't screw up again," Handel said. "But who's to say it will work out the way it's supposed to?"

Billie wiped her eyes and pulled away. "It doesn't matter. As long as we get Davy back, it will be worth it."

"Where are you supposed to bring them, Handel?" Margaret asked.

"I don't know."

"What do you mean, you don't know? He said in the note…"

He threw up his hands. "I know what he wrote, but I'm telling you that I don't know what he meant. I've gone round and round it in my head. Cut corners and skip steps! What does that even mean? Maybe he was messing with me again, seeing if I'd report it to the police—I don't know."

"You know him better than anybody else here," Billie said, moving toward him. She took his hands and looked into his face. "Think. Where is he the most comfortable? Where would he feel safe?" Her eyes widened. "Where did you cut corners and skip steps?"

"The woodworking shed. He slept there, worked there," he paused, "took most of the girls there."

Adam shook his head. "We searched all of the buildings. It didn't look like anybody had been in that building for months."

"The equipment is still there and once in a while somebody uses it to fix something around here, but mostly it's just used for storage now," Billie confirmed.

"That doesn't mean my father wouldn't go back there. I think we should try it." Margaret bit her lip and waited, hoping they would agree.

Handel stared at her for a long moment and then nodded. "We don't have any other choice. If Billie is willing to release the pictures, then we have to try. I'll leave them there this evening after everyone goes home."

"What about the police?" Margaret asked. "We have to let them in on it. We can't do it alone. They have the man power to set a wide enough net to catch him."

"I'll talk to them. They already think I'm withholding information, so this should come as no surprise to them," he said, his voice caustic.

"I'm coming with you." Billie followed him to the door. At his look of surprise, she smiled and took his hand. "It's not your job to explain why I kept the photographs in my possession. I should do that myself."

"Good luck," Adam said.

"I don't believe in luck anymore, little brother. Try a prayer. It'll go a lot farther.

CHAPTER FOURTEEN

Adam maneuvered the forklift under the grape bin and backed up, slowly turned and moved toward the sorter. Leo stood at the top waiting. He wiped his forehead with the back of his shirt sleeve and grinned, yelled something to one of the other men working the belt. Adam tipped the load, letting it pour in.

He backed up the forklift, spun it around and set the empty bin back on the trailer. Loren waved from the seat of the tractor and moved out, the trailer of empty bins following along behind. Adam parked the forklift off to the side of the yard, out of the way of incoming traffic and hopped down.

Nearly all the grapes had been brought in, except for Margaret's field. Loren was going out to bring in the rest of what had been picked, and then the crew would come in for lunch. He looked up at the sky from under the bill of his cap. The sun was nearly straight up. It had already been a long day and it was only noon. He couldn't remember the last time he was so tired. He blew out a weary sigh, pulled his cap off, scratched his head and slapped it back on again. He was beginning to think accounting might just be his dream job after all.

"Hey, Adam!" called one of the women working the belt. "Come're!"

The twenty-something Mexican girl had been flirting outrageously with him every time he was within smiling distance. He thought her name was Juanita, but he wasn't sure. She stood on the other side of the belt picking through the grapes that came down the line, throwing out any leaves, debris, or bad fruit that got left from the sorter. All the castoff was thrown into the large bin by the wall.

"What's up?" he asked, approaching the belt.

The girl gestured with her head toward the nearly full bin. "Could you bring the forklift around the building and take that away? The flies are driving me crazy!"

"Sure. I'll ask Billie where she wants me to dump it."

"Gracias." She wrinkled her nose. "I hate flies. They remind me of death. I had a pet lamb when I was a girl. A wild dog came during the night and ripped a hole in its side. In the morning, maggots were in the wound, and then flies were everywhere. It was horrible. My father had to shoot it." She shook her head, black shoulder-length hair swaying with the motion. "Flies disgust me!"

Adam stared at the girl, his mind locked on her first words. *I hate flies. They remind me of death.* She smiled seductively and batted her eyelashes as though they had a serious connection. He peered over her shoulder, his gaze moving to the bin six feet behind her. Sure enough, a cloud of flies hovered, darted, landed and dove into the cast off fruit. He swallowed hard, remembering what Margaret had said just days ago, "We'll never be free of him until he's dead." Had she gotten her wish? If so, where was Davy in all of this?

Juanita's flirty expression disappeared. She was suddenly all business, her eyes on the belt and the fruit coming down the line. She picked out a bad grape and piece of stem, tossing them into the small bin at her feet. Adam turned around. Margaret was walking toward them, her eyes narrowed with interest. She stopped to chat with one of the other girls working the belt.

He hurried to her side and took her arm, turning her the other direction. "Meg, I need to talk to you," he said.

"Hold on. I haven't spoken with Juanita yet. Someone is not keeping their eyes on the belt. I can't have bad grapes making it through the line to the press." She glanced toward the girl in question, her lips thinning into a disapproving line. "Billie said she had problems with her last year. She's too busy flirting with the guys to take the job seriously."

"Really? I hadn't noticed," he lied, trying once again to pull her away from the yard. He didn't think learning her father was buried in a bin of rotten fruit would be a highlight to the day even if she did hate him.

She certainly didn't need to be here when they found out for sure. "I'll speak with her later, but I really need to talk to you now."

"All right. Talk." She pulled away from his grip and crossed her arms over her chest. "What's going on?"

"Nothing," he said, glancing toward the bin. "It's personal."

She followed his gaze and apparently thought he was staring at Juanita. Her eyes widened and she released a sound of disgust. "You've got to be kidding."

"No." He put up his hands in defense. "Not that kind of personal."

She didn't appear convinced.

"It's about your father."

"You know what? I've had enough talk about my father." She pushed past him and mad a beeline for Juanita. "Right now I want to focus on work."

He stayed back and watched her. She said something to Juanita and gestured toward the opening where the grapes entered the winery and were introduced into the press. The girl kept her eyes down, focused on the job at hand, only glancing up and nodding once or twice while Margaret berated her. When the girl inclined her head toward the bin and said something with that *ick* look on her face, Adam moved quickly forward.

"Juanita said you were going to take care of the bin back there," Margaret said, hands on her hips. "Why aren't you doing it?"

"I need to ask Billie where she wants it dumped," he said. "You want to come with me?"

She looked at him as though he'd lost his mind. "Why don't you just take it back there by the compost pile? You don't need to bother Billie with that."

"Oh. Okay. I'll do that."

"Good." She stared at him until he turned and went back to the forklift.

He climbed in and started it, jerked forward toward the parking area, forks lifted. He glanced back. She had crawled under the belt and was standing on the other side now. The side where the bin sat. He turned around in time to keep from running over Ernesto. "Sorry!" he yelled, as the man jumped out of the way.

He drove the machine through the gravel parking area, between the buildings and behind the winery. The rutted road made the machine bump and jerk even more than usual. He whacked his head on the roof a couple of times. He turned at the corner of the building, right where the bin should be, and jerked to a stop, his foot hitting the brake with enough force to eject him if he hadn't been holding on tight.

A group of workers were huddled around Margaret where she lay crumpled on the ground. Juanita squatted beside her holding her wrist, as though checking for a pulse. Margaret's eyes were closed and she wasn't moving.

Adam jumped from the forklift and pushed through the onlookers. He dropped to his knees beside Margaret, lifted her in his arms and made his way around the machinery to the front of the building. Someone had already run to call for help. Sally met him at the door of the winery.

"What happened?"

"I think she fainted." He carried her through the door, held open by Sally, and into the conference room. The smell of stale coffee and new carpet pervaded the room. He hooked one of the chairs with his foot and rolled it out from the table. He carefully settled her in the chair and laid her head atop the table, gently patted her cheek.

"Here." Sally held out a glass of water.

"What do you want me to do with that?" he asked, setting it on the table. "Poor it over her head? Unconscious people can't swallow."

"You don't have to bite Sally's head off. She's just trying to help," his sister said, rushing into the room with Handel beside her.

"Sorry."

"What happened?" Handel demanded. "We pulled up and saw you carrying her."

"Mmmmm," Margaret stirred. Her eyes opened and she slowly raised her head and looked around the room, confused. Then something clicked and she screamed, "Davy! The bin. He's in the bin!"

Adam shook his head. "No, that can't be. It's not Davy. It can't be Davy."

"I saw him. The hat he wore." She broke down and wept, her head in her hands.

Adam looked at Billie, and shook his head. "No." He ran from the room and down the hall, shoved open the front door and gasped for breath. He felt like the air had all been sucked from his lungs, leaving nothing but emptiness and dread.

Two news vans were still parked in the gravel lot, staying back from the wine-making operation, but close enough to be on the spot if something went down. Like vultures they hovered, waiting for the story to break so they could broadcast someone else's pain on national television and ask, "*How does it feel?*" The sliding doors were open and the two cameramen were already grabbing their gear. As if in a race, one reporter touched up her makeup and patted her hair in place, looking in the side mirror, while the reporter from the competing station shrugged into a suit coat and straightened his tie.

Adam hurried around the side of the building and back to the work yard. Everyone had returned to their jobs as though nothing happened, as though there were no body rotting in a bin of rotten fruit. What was wrong with people?

Juanita glanced up from her work. "Is Miss Parker all right?" she asked.

"How can you ask that? Of course she's not all right. She just saw…" he broke off and looked around the yard at the curious faces staring back. Not one looked as though they'd seen a dead body, especially not the body of a little boy they'd all been searching for, for the last two days.

"What did she see?"

He crawled under the belt and went to the bin. Waved the flies away and looked inside. Part of a baseball cap stuck up through smashed grapes and litter, the bill turned purple with juice but the logo still readable. *Golden Gate Racetrack*

He heard a commotion and looked up. The reporters, cameramen in tow, approached the yard looking for the story. He jumped in the forklift and started the engine. The machine roared to life and he dropped the fork, moved forward to position them under the bin and brought up the lever to lift. The news people could obviously smell a story. They headed his way, cameras rolling, microphones out.

He heard a crash and turned around. In his rush to get away, he hadn't positioned the bin solidly on the forks. The box had tipped and everything came pouring out. Including the body of Agosto Salvatore.

***

The police cordoned off the yard, now a crime scene, thoroughly shutting down the winemaking operation for the day. Statements were taken, endless questions were asked, and finally the workers were told to go home. The reporters were pushed back to the parking area, but they'd already gotten the sensational story they hoped for. A dead body fermenting in a bin of rotten grapes was titillating news in wine country. Competition was fierce with wine growers, but murder took it to a whole new level. The fact that Agosto Salvatore had nothing to do with Fredrickson Winery didn't really matter. He died there during harvest and Fredrickson's was struggling financially. They mentioned the kidnapping as though perhaps it were all part of a diabolical plan to extort money from Salvatore to keep the winery up and running.

The officers they spoke with before were low men on the totem pole now. Two detectives from homicide showed up to take over the case. Adam was taken downtown and questioned repeatedly. After all, he did find the body and reported a gunshot the night before that no one else seemed to have heard. He thought they must be taking their cues from the six o'clock news rather than reality.

"I already told the other officers. I don't know how he got there. It was dark last night. I wasn't close enough to see anything. I showed Officer Stanton some marks on the ground. I thought they looked like something had been dragged across the yard toward the bin, but he didn't think it was important." He threw up his hands. "Why aren't you out looking for Sean Parker? He's the child molester, kidnapper, and now murderer."

Detective Olson tapped the table with his index finger. "Why did you run out there to move the bin when Miss Parker said she thought her son was in there? Sounds like guilt to me."

"You've got to kidding!"

"We don't kid about murder, Mr. Fredrickson."

With elbows propped on the interrogation room table, he dropped his head in hands and repeated once again, "I saw the reporters running to get a story. I couldn't let Margaret suffer more. If Davy really was in that bin, I had to move it. She wouldn't want people staring at her little boy—like that. Taking pictures, video. So I tried to move the bin, but I screwed up."

"Did you screw up, Mr. Fredrickson?" The detective raised one brow. "Or did you dump it on purpose to taint the evidence?"

He groaned. "You've been watching too many cop shows, detective. I was just trying to save my friend a little heartache."

"Well, it seems someone did that by killing the father of her son, who coincidentally just happened to have a pack of lawyers working on paternity and custody claims on his behalf."

He remained silent, refusing to dig himself in further by arguing the validity of such claims on the part of Agosto Salvatore. The man was dead and someone shot him. The police didn't care at this point whether he was worthy of a place on the FBI's most wanted list, or a potential recipient of the father of the year award, they just wanted to nail someone for his murder so they could check the box on their paperwork—case closed.

"You can go now," the detective said, moving away from the table. He pulled open the door and stood there, waiting.

Adam narrowed his gaze. "That's it?"

"Unless you want to confess."

He got up, scooting back the chair and walked out.

Billie was waiting for him. She'd obviously played her lawyer card and got him released. She pulled him into her arms. "Do you know how much trouble I'd be in if Mother found out I let you get arrested?"

He pulled back and grinned. "They didn't arrest me."

"Yeah, well they were this close." She held up her hand, her thumb and forefinger barely a fraction apart. "I had to threaten them with criminal lawyer speak and believe me I have no idea what I'm doing. I'm a family lawyer, for heaven sake. Handel should be here."

"I'm glad you came. Mom would be proud."

"I'd rather she never found out."

"That might be wishful thinking," he said, his tone grim. "Remember the news vans? A kidnapping and murder all at a California winery? No doubt it's going national."

She groaned.

"How's Margaret doing?" he asked, following her out of the police station.

"She's dealing with the fact that finding out Agosto was dead instead of Davy was the happiest moment of her life." She opened the car door and looked at him across the hood. "That's a lot to digest. Relief—even joy—is a natural human reaction when something like this happens, but then guilt sets in. She'll be struggling with lots of conflicting feelings for a long time."

He nodded, knowing she spoke from experience. "And we haven't even found Davy yet."

"No, but Handel is working on it."

They drove back to the winery mostly in silence. The police had insisted the news vans leave the premises, so when they turned down the drive the parking area was eerily empty, except for Handel's, Margaret's and Sally's cars.

Margaret's promise to give Jane Goodall an exclusive interview had been postponed due to circumstances and everyone was relieved about that— including Jane Goodall who seemed on the verge of tears after Salvatore's body was discovered. She'd apparently gotten more than she bargained for in that relationship.

Margaret and Handel were in the front office with Sally when they arrived. Adam hesitated outside the door, afraid Margaret might have some of the same doubts the police had about why he did what he did. She broke off mid-sentence from speaking with Sally and flew to the door to embrace him.

"Are you all right? I was so worried that the police were going to arrest you. They had no business taking you downtown like you were a common criminal."

He pressed his forehead to hers and smiled. "That's right. If I were a criminal I would certainly not be common."

"Exactly."

"If you two are done playing kissy face," Sally said, moving toward the doorway with her purse in hand. "I have to leave. The police don't want any random people around to accidentally get shot or something.

That means me." She stopped and looked around at them all, her eyes suspiciously moist. "See you tomorrow."

When Sally was gone, Handel picked up the packet of Polaroid pictures that Billie had retrieved from her office safe earlier and the thick ten thousand dollar bundle of cash he'd withdrawn from the bank. "As soon as it's dark, I'm going to take these to the shed and leave them on the work bench in plain sight. The police will be staking out the building from a good distance so as not to alert him when he comes to pick up the money and photos," he said. "We're supposed to stay inside out of the way. But I'm not going to let something happen to Davy because they drop the ball again." He opened his jacket and pulled out a small handgun. "When it comes to my father, the only thing he understands is force."

"Where did you get that?" Margaret asked, shocked. "I thought we only had the one gun and he took it."

"I've had a conceal/carry license for a few years. For protection. I didn't tell you because I didn't want you to worry. I keep it at the office mostly. Some of the people I deal with make threats now and then."

"What are you saying, Handel?" Billie asked. "You know better than anyone that taking the law into your own hands is a mistake. We have to have faith that evil will be repaid, that justice will be dispensed. We can't do it ourselves."

"I can't believe you're the one saying that. After what he did to you…"

"You can't make what happened to me null and void by doing something that will only bring more pain. I love you," she said, and from the look on his face it was the first time she'd said it out loud.

Margaret pulled Adam out the doorway. "Let's take a walk."

The evening settled in, deepening patches of shadow under the trees and along the buildings. The last rays of sunlight, dingy pink, melted into the horizon. Adam twined his fingers with Margaret's and they moved toward the vineyard. A squirrel scampered across fallen leaves and disappeared up the trunk of an oak with a swish of tail.

"Billie's changed a lot since she's been here," he said, plucking a red leaf from the vines beside him. He twirled it by the stem. "For the better. She's a lot more open. I think Handel is really good for her. I had my doubts a few days ago, but she actually said the words—in front of us, no less." He laughed, a slow chuckle that built to a snort. "She probably hates that she did that. But I'm glad. It shows she's human. When I was a kid, sometimes I wondered."

"She couldn't have been that bad."

"No. She was a good sister. Just a little bottled up. Her and my mother have had a strained relationship over the years, but I think its getting better. I hope so, cause I got a voice mail from Mom that said she was flying out here in the morning."

"You didn't tell Billie, did you?"

He took a deep breath and released it. "Nope."

"You are in trouble."

"Yep."

They walked a little ways farther and then he stopped and pulled her into his arms. "It's going to be all right, Meg. You'll see Davy tonight."

She wrapped her arms around him and clung, silent as the moon.

***

When they returned, Billie was sitting at the desk, the pictures of the girls spread out before her like Taro cards. Handel silently watched from his chair across the desk. Margaret and Adam hovered in the doorway, unsure about what was going on.

Billie looked up and smiled sheepishly. "Just in case we don't get them back," she said, as though she'd been memorizing their faces. She tapped each one in turn. "This is Sarah—gone now. Lori." She picked it up, looking closely at the face of the girl in the faded Polaroid. "I haven't been able to find out anything about her…" She set that one down and touched the next, "or Tina. Except I think Tina's mother worked here at one time. Ernesto remembered a girl who came with her mother, but I don't know what year that was. He's worked here since Jack bought the winery. " She moved to the next. "Cindy lives in Los Angeles with a boyfriend. From what she shared over the telephone, it sounded like an abusive relationship. Angie is a nurse in Seattle. She's married with three kids. She was very

233

happy when I told her last year that our abuser was in prison, but she said she'd moved on and didn't want to come forward at the time. Who knows what she'd say now." The last photo she looked at for a second without saying anything.

She slowly gathered them back into a pile and slid them into the envelope, set it atop the bundle of money and pushed it toward Handel. "We're ready."

Handel picked up a two-way and spoke into it. "I'm delivering the package now."

An answer came back, "Ten four."

"The police didn't wire you?" Adam asked.

"I asked them not to. If I do run into my father out there he's paranoid enough to search me. I don't want him to have an excuse to back out on his promise. He may be an evil man but he usually stands by his word. I'm praying this time it'll hold true." He picked up the bundles and kissed Billie. The gun lay deserted on the corner of the desk. "Be right back."

"Be careful, Handel," Margaret said, her throat tight.

He smiled and turned to go.

Adam followed and watched from the front door. Handel walked swiftly across the parking area and disappeared into the shrubbery and trees that surrounded the equipment and woodworking sheds. Soon a light flicked on in the shed and then moments later went out again. So far so good.

Handel was back in the winery within minutes. He ran his fingers nervously through his hair. "The ball is in his court. I hope he's watching. Now all we can do is wait."

The radio crackled every fifteen minutes. No sign of him.

Margaret paced from the office, down the hall, into the tasting room and back again. On her third circuitous route, Adam joined her and stopped to peruse the black and white photographs lining the far wall. He hadn't taken any notice of them before, but he was obviously trying to distract her for a few moments.

"Is this Davy?" he asked, although the picture was old. He bent close to the glass to block the glare of the overhead lights. His look of chagrin told her that he probably just realized it wasn't the best way to distract her from worry about Davy.

"No, that's my father when he was a little boy." Margaret pointed at the farmer behind him, a droopy felt hat covering half his face. "And that's my grandfather. I never met him. He died long before I was born. Lung cancer."

He moved on to the next picture. A Mexican family with five children stood under a sign over the winery that read, *Wines of Sanchez*. "I know this probably sounds prejudice, like I think Mexicans all look alike or something, but have you noticed how this man looks a lot like Mario?"

Margaret was still intent on her father's photograph. "What do you think happens to someone to turn him from a sweet, innocent child into a monster?" she asked, looking up into his face.

"I don't know."

She slowly turned her gaze to the other picture, feeling as though she was coming out of a daze. "What did you say about Mario?"

"I know he's too young to be the elder Mr. Sanchez in this picture, but he looks enough like him to be his twin. You think he's related? Like maybe one of his kids. This boy would probably be about Mario's age now."

She bent close. "Is that a scar on his forehead?"

"Looks like a scar."

"Mario has a scar on his forehead. He usually keeps it covered with a bandana or his hat. That is a weird coincidence." She moved away from the wall, but glanced back, a little frown between her brows. "Really weird."

"So, you don't think I'm being prejudice?" He grinned.

"No, but I think you're a sweet guy for trying to take my mind off things."

"I can live with that."

When they returned to the office, Billie and Handel still sat silently, lost in their own thoughts. The big clock on the wall ticked loudly in the small room, reminding everyone that two hours had passed since the drop off and the police had no sighting of Sean Parker picking up the package.

Margaret dropped into the metal folding chair and leaned forward, elbows on her knees, head in her hands. "I can't take much more," she said.

"Want anything from the snack machine?" Adam asked from the doorway.

No one responded, so he leaned against the wall and crossed his arms.

Margaret's cell phone started playing the tune to *I'm a Believer*, and she jumped. She fumbled in her sweatshirt pocket and pulled it out, flipped it open. "Yes?"

"Hello, Maggie."

"Dad?" She didn't want to call him that, but what else could she call him? He was holding her son hostage and offending him was the last thing she wanted to do. She said, in desperation, "Where's Davy? Is he all right? Please, you have to give him back."

"That's why I called. I decided I can't hurt my baby girl anymore. I've been a selfish bastard up to now. I know you probably don't believe me, but I want to turn over a new leaf." He stopped to cough and then drew a raspy breath before he continued. "Davy's just fine. I wouldn't do anything to hurt him. He's my grandson."

"Then where is he, Dad? Please tell me." Her hand shook as she held the phone close to her ear. She glanced at the others in the room and nodded, her eyes wide. "Handel left the pictures and money in the woodworking building. Please—take them! Just bring Davy home."

There was a lengthy pause, and she thought she heard the sound of a door closing and the crunch of gravel.

"Well that's just it, Maggie. I decided I'm not taking those things. After what happened with Salvatore, the cops are gonna be on me like lice on a chicken. Can't afford to come back for that little bit of money. Besides, Salvatore already paid me enough to live on for awhile."

"What do you mean, come back? You left and took Davy with you?" She tried to tone down her voice but she was on the verge of screaming.

"Settle down now, Maggie. Davy is right where I left him. In your tool shed by the Parker vineyard. He's fine—just a little tipsy from your homemade wine. I had to give him that to keep him quiet, cause Salvatore gave me horse pills to give my grandson. That's why I shot him. He didn't tell me about the side effects. Davy could've choked to death if I hadn't found him in time. That man deserved to die. What kind of a father would ask a kidnapper to give his own son horse tranquilizers?"

She covered the phone with her hand and whispered. "Tell the police Davy's in *my* tool shed, Handel. Dad left him there and skipped town." She put the phone back to her ear. He was still talking about Salvatore.

"…can see why you hated him. I did you a favor, Maggie. I guess you owe me one."

She started to argue but the line went dead.

"He's gone," she said, and flipped the phone closed.

Handel was already out the door, radio in hand. She could hear him relaying the information to the police and their crackling response. Everyone was converging on the Parker shed.

She ran out after him, Adam and Billie following close on her heels. Handel's car was too small for all of them, so they piled into Margaret's. Handel drove, whipping around in the gravel like a teenager on a joyride. She hoped and prayed that it would be exactly that.

The house, yard, and shed were awash with the glare of headlights when they arrived. Undercover cops swarmed over the area, a team of synchronized killers, surrounding the shed, fully armed. Margaret saw one man go in and then another. Others stood outside the door, guns drawn.

The first officer finally emerged through the door of the shed, Davy's small body in his arms. He smiled broadly, blinking against the lights in his eyes, and strode forward. Margaret ran to meet him, tears coursing down her cheeks. She lifted Davy's arm, hanging limply, and squeezed his fingers, pressing them to her lips. He giggled, and opened his eyes. They were bloodshot, but his silly smile made her laugh along.

Handel stepped forward and took him from the officer. "We should get him in the house."

"I'm sure someone's already called for an ambulance. It's best if he gets checked out by a doctor. You don't know what he's been given."

Margaret ran a finger along her son's cheek and kissed his forehead. "He's been given homemade Wine," she said, with a shake of her head. "Not fatal, but he's definitely tipsy."

Handel carried him in and laid him on the couch. Margaret covered him with the quilt and sat on the floor beside him, her arm protectively over his chest. He turned his head to look at her, their eyes on the same level, and then they slowly drooped closed and he began to snore.

Margaret looked up to see Handel still hovering nearby. Billie and Adam stood in the kitchen speaking with two policemen. She closed her eyes and breathed a prayer of thanksgiving.

***

Handel drove Billie and Adam back to the winery once everything settled down. Davy had been checked out by the EMT, and the police had taped off the shed as a crime scene and finally dispersed. The highway was a dark stretch of inky black in the light of the Toyota's headlights. No other cars in sight. He turned onto the long gravel drive and glanced at Billie in the seat beside him.

"Margaret wouldn't leave him alone in his room tonight," he said, his voice soft. "She was curled up on the bed beside him."

"I don't blame her." Billie reached out and ran her fingers through the hair at the nape of his neck in a gentle caress. "It'll take some time to get past this."

He nodded.

Adam watched from the backseat, saying nothing. He didn't want to break the mood of joyful relief. Everything had turned out well in the end, thank God, other than putting Sean Parker back behind bars where he belonged, but hopefully the police would remedy that soon.

Handel parked under the oaks and they all got out and walked down to the woodworking shed to retrieve the money and pictures. The door was open, hinges creaking as it moved ever so slightly in the breeze. "What the…" Handel muttered and flipped the light switch. The room came to life with bright overhead florescent bulbs. The smell of freshly cut pine pervaded the room along with a hint of cigarette smoke.

A table saw and a circular saw built into their own cutting tables, took up much of the open floor space. One long wall held wood working tools of every description. Adam spotted handsaws, levels, planes, awls, a shaver, and things he didn't recognize. The floor was covered in a fine powder of sawdust and curling wood shavings.

On the worktable sat a small pine birdhouse.

Handel shook his head. "I don't believe it," he said, his eyes wide with wonder. "The bastard tricked us. Somehow he knew the exact moment I left the package. And he knew everyone would desert the stakeout as soon as he called and told Margaret where Davy was. He made us believe he'd already left town, when he was right outside our door waiting." He met

Billie's eyes across the room, his own guilt-ridden. "I'm sorry. He took the pictures."

Adam looked up at the ceiling and around the door and windowsill. He felt along the edges of the tables with his fingers, feeling for something that didn't belong.

"What are you looking for?" Billie asked, coming up behind him where he crouched to look under the bottom of the cutting table. "He took the pictures and the money. It's over."

He found the object, yanked it off the wood where it had been taped in place and lifted it up for inspection. "How did he know when we left and how long we'd be gone? Because he was watching."

Handel reached out to take it from him. The camera was about the size of his thumb. He turned it over in his hand. "How did you know?"

He shrugged. "A friend at college was a wannabe private investigator. He was always buying these tiny gadgets and spying on people. That looks like one he had—motion detection and a 72 degree angle view. Your dad just needed a laptop computer nearby and he could watch the show without anyone being the wiser." He crossed his arms. "He was one step ahead of us the whole time. I'm sure he planted a camera in the shed where Davy was too. Maybe even in your house. His little game of breaking and entering probably involved more than just taking the gun and leaving Pablo."

Handel handed the tiny camera back to Adam and approached the workbench. He lifted the newly built birdhouse, looked inside and underneath, felt the smooth wood with his fingertips. "He actually built this while half a mile away a dozen cops stormed our shed with enough commotion and light to wake the Napa Valley. Just to prove he's better than me—without cutting corners or skipping steps—even under pressure.

CHAPTER FIFTEEN

Adam yawned and stretched, padding out of his room in bare feet. He cinched the string on his sweats and looked around for his running shoes. He couldn't remember where he'd left them. He carried his socks to the kitchen. Maybe they were by the back door.

Billie was already up nibbling on toast and drinking coffee. He looked greedily at her second slice, but she moved the plate to the other side of the newspaper she was reading, out of his reach. "We made front page news," she announced. She didn't sound excited about it.

He found his shoes and sat down at the table to pull on his socks. "What'd you expect? Kidnapping and murder are still pretty newsworthy even in California. Jane Goodall and the five o'clock news will be up and running with her exclusive interview before you know it. She's probably pulling Margaret out of bed as we speak."

"I hope not. Ernesto said they were going over to harvest her vineyard this morning. Knowing her, she's out there helping even though I told her to take time off. She could use a few hours rest and relaxation after the past few days, spend a little quiet time with Davy, and then if she has to, come in later this afternoon to supervise the winemaking."

He grinned, double knotting his shoes. "Dream on. She's sort of one-track minded like yourself." He got up and opened the back door. "Got to run. See you in thirty."

He walked briskly along the back of the house, following the paver stones that wound past the rose bushes and around the side to the gravel drive. He hadn't run enough since he'd been here and his body felt out of tune. He started at a slow jog, heading toward the highway, then broke into a run. The cool morning air felt good against his bare chest. A stray cat pounced on something in the tall grass of the ditch he passed. Further down the road, he heard tapping and looked up to see a woodpecker looking for bugs in the bark of an old olive tree, long black beak above a little tufted red head hammering away like a rock and roll drummer.

He turned after about two miles and started back. He would like to go further but Billie would need him back at the winery soon. There was much left to be done. He heard a car approaching from behind and moved onto the shoulder, barely staying out of the ditch. This was a dangerous road most days, pedestrians and bicyclers were warned to be alert. Wineries and driving didn't mix well. But since the wineries were closed for harvest he hoped he was safe enough.

The car sped past, a little silver Ford Taurus. It slowed, brake lights coming on, and then pulled over to the side of the road. He watched the car as he approached, wondering if they were lost. When he neared, the window rolled down and a woman looked out at him, perfectly coifed brown hair framing his mother's lovely frown.

"What are you doing out here half dressed, Adam?" She glanced up and down the road. "Get in this car before someone sees you."

He sighed and hurried across the road. No matter how old he got, there was no arguing with Mom. He climbed into the car, still panting.

"Now don't get any sweat on these cloth seats. This is a rental, you know."

"Yes, Mother," he said, as sweat dripped down his face and chest and soaked into the seat at his back.

"You are certainly ripe," she commented, turning up her nose and putting the car into gear. She left the window open even though she hated her hair getting windblown and pulled back out on the road to drive the remaining distance. With her blinker on for the turn into Fredrickson's she asked, "You did tell Billie I was coming, right?"

He prayed that Billie, still basking in the joy of finding Davy safe and sound, would forgive him for neglecting to pass on this small tidbit of news—Mother had come for a visit.

"With everything that's been going on, I really haven't had a chance," he said, wishing he'd worn a shirt so he could wipe away the sweat dripping in his eyes.

She shook her head. "I heard all about it at the airport this morning. Saw that blonde woman on channel five report that Sean Parker released his grandson and disappeared into thin air." She glanced his way, her lips pursed with concern. "How's Billie doing? Knowing he's out running loose has got to be very frustrating for her. Not to mention, frightening."

"She's managing," he said.

She parked the car in front of the house and shut off the ignition. Adam glanced up at the front windows, wondering if Billie had spotted them yet. He opened the door and got out, looked down at the damp seat he left behind and hoped his mother wouldn't notice. He quickly went around the car and opened her door, standing back as she gathered her purse.

She gestured toward the trunk. "Get my things, will you honey? I'll surprise Billie. She is still home, isn't she?" She glanced at her little diamond studded watch his father had given her decades ago. "I took the earliest flight available so I could be here for her."

He popped the trunk and struggled to extract the giant suitcase she'd managed to cram into the small space. It weighed more than she did. He wondered how she ever got it to the airport and then into the trunk without suffering a hernia. "It is harvest, Mom. So, she may have gone to the winery already."

She hurried up the front walk, knocked and rang the bell, patted at her hair, and tried to peek through the front window. He pulled the suitcase down the sidewalk, glad it had wheels, but thinking it should include a motor as well. "Just open it, Mom. It's not locked."

Her expression was aghast. "Not locked? After everything that's happened—she doesn't lock her doors?"

He sighed and followed her in, yanking the suitcase up over the steps and through the doorway. A loud crash reverberated from the kitchen, followed by loud muttering. Apparently Billie had spotted their guest. He closed the door behind him and locked it.

***

Margaret hovered over Davy while he ate enough food to rival his uncle Handel's appetite. She brushed her fingers lightly over his head every time she passed by his chair, needing that small physical contact to reinforce the fact that he was home and safe.

"I want to go see Pablo. Is he all right? Grandpa Sean didn't hurt him, did he?" he asked, after finishing his second glass of orange juice. It was the first he'd mentioned his friend, and was a good sign that he was not devastated by the past few days, blocking out bad memories, but that the drug and alcohol had actually caused his time in confinement to seem short and not nearly as scary as it could have. He still didn't know what happened to his father and Margaret thought it might be too soon to bring it up.

"I don't know if Pablo has been back to the winery. We'll have to call his parents and see if we can stop at their place for a visit soon. But today Ernesto and the crew is out harvesting the Parker vines and I think we should be involved in that, don't you?"

Davy nodded, a grin spreading across his face. "Your new wine blend will be the best ever!" he said with all the confidence of a nine-year-old connoisseur.

"Now you're talking. Brush your teeth, Mr. Parker, so we can get going."

He made a face. "Do I got to? I'm just going to dirty 'em up when I eat grapes out there anyway."

"You better keep your mitts off my grapes, buddy. Those grapes are meant for wine making, not snacking." She smacked the seat of his pants. "Go on."

The phone rang. She set Davy's dirty dishes in the sink and picked up.

"Miss Parker?"

"I'll be out to help in a minute, Ernesto."

"Okay, but I was just wondering if you'd heard from Mario since he took Pablo home the other day. I tried to call the number but he doesn't answer."

Margaret couldn't remember seeing the man since then either. Funny that no one mentioned it before now. If anyone should be holding down the fort it would be the two vineyard managers. "Why don't you call Billie. She might have another contact number in the employee files."

Davy trudged back into the room, wearing the hat his father gave him with the Golden Gate Racetrack insignia. She cringed at the thought that only recently she'd believed him dead, buried in that bin of rotten fruit, his cap sticking up through the muck. She turned away, so he wouldn't see the horror she felt at the thought. "Don't you think you should wear an old cap, so you don't get that one dirty?" she suggested.

He pulled it off and looked at it, his bottom lip caught between his front teeth. "I guess. I'll get my Star Wars hat. Be right back!" He ran up the stairs to his room. When he returned, he was wearing a black cap, glow-in-the-dark sabers crossed on the front.

Margaret hugged him and he suffered through it once again, pretending he was too big to hug. "Aw, Mom."

***

Billie and Adam escaped to the winery while their mother freshened up from her travel. After that long flight, practically in the middle of the night, she said she needed to rest. Relieved at the respite, they hurried back to work.

Sally was already at her desk, her face beaming when Adam came in. "I knew everything would turn out. I'm so happy for Margaret. Davy is home safe and sound and now we can all get back to normal," she said.

"If you don't mind the fact that Sean Parker is still running loose," Adam said, bending over the front of her desk. He ran his fingers along the edges and then bent down to look around the bottom.

"What are you doing? Looking for used gum?"

He raised his head and met her curious stare. "I'm looking for bugs."

"Ick! We don't allow bugs in the winery, and certainly not on my desk."

"A different kind of bug. You know—the kind that listens to other people's conversations? Sort of like you, only smaller and technologically advanced."

"Holy Moly! Have you lost your mind? Why would someone bug the winery?" she got up and moved around her desk to watch him feeling along the legs of the chairs.

He flipped one chair and then the other, checking under the seats, then righted them again. He put his finger to his lips. "You never know who's listening."

Billie appeared in the doorway, frowning. "What are you doing on the floor?"

He looked up and grinned. "Cleaning house?"

She'd obviously overheard. "There are no bugs in the winery. The lock pad on the front door is changed every month and only Sally, Ernesto, Mario, and I have the combination. I haven't even had time to give it to Margaret. Handel said they did find a camera in the Parker shed though and one taped under the table in Margaret's cellar, so Sean would know when we found Pablo. The police didn't find any bugs."

He shrugged and stood up. "Can't be too careful."

Sally rolled her eyes and released an exaggerated sigh. She went back to the computer on her desk and started typing.

"Sally, do we have more than one phone number for Mario? Ernesto hasn't been able to reach him with the one he has."

"I'll look."

Adam stood over her shoulder and watched as she opened the employee files, clicking on Mario Nava. There was one cell phone number and his emergency contact person. She looked up. "Just his emergency contact number. Do you want that? It's his sister. Carlita Ortiz."

Billie bit her lip. "That must be Pablo's mother. Send me an email with the number, would you? I'll call them in a bit. I need to talk to Handel first."

Adam followed her down the hall to her office. He could tell she was worried about something. "What's up? You're not still mad about Mom showing up? It's not my fault," he said, his defenses up.

"No. Nobody can control Mother's flights of fancy." She sat back behind the desk and picked up the phone. "Something has been nagging at the back of my mind. Handel told me that before they released Sean Parker on probation, he had two people vouch for him. I find it hard to believe that random citizens would vouch for a sex offender unless there was some ulterior motive. I want to know what their names are."

"You think it's someone you know?" He was truly surprised. He leaned over her desk, his palms flat on the surface.

She dialed the number and waited. "Handel? Did you ever find out the names of the people who went before Sean's probation hearing? Yes. Could you? Thanks." She held a hand over the mouthpiece. "He has a friend who works over there. He's calling them on the other line."

Adam slumped on his tailbone in the chair behind him and waited, hands clasped behind his head. His sister looked grim, tapping her pen against the desktop in an agitated manner. He wondered what Sean Parker's probation hearing had to do with their missing vineyard manager. The night he'd followed Salvatore to the winery, she'd been adamant that none of her employees could possibly be involved in Davy's kidnapping. He was sure she would have vouched for each and every one of them at the time—but now?

She tipped the phone back against her ear. "Yes. Juan and Carlita Ortiz. Did anyone happen to check them out? See if they were legal citizens?" She scribbled something on a scrap of paper. "I know. California's policy is don't ask, don't tell. Well I'm asking for a reason. Carlita is Mario's sister and he hasn't been seen or heard from since he took Pablo home. Don't you find that coincidence a bit disturbing, seeing as your father got away?" She paused and listened, then added, "Maybe he had help."

When she hung up, Adam leaned forward, his chin in his hands. "What motive could Mario possibly have to help Parker? His file said you hired him a year ago. Long before Parker was released by the parole board."

She looked down at the note and shook her head. "I don't know. But I think his sister does."

"What if she won't talk to you?"

Her eyes widened and she smiled. "We have a secret weapon. Davy. I'm sure Pablo would want to see that his friend is safe and sound." She picked up the phone again.

"Are you calling Carlita Ortiz?"

"No. I'm calling Margaret. She can set it up to appear like an innocent play date."

"You're pretty sneaky."

She turned her swivel chair to face away from him. "Margaret?"

***

"This is it." Margaret squinted at the stenciled numbers on the beat up mailbox. It looked like someone had driven over it and then set it back up in the hole again. The post leaned West like a drunken cowboy.

Billie pulled the car over and parked at the curb. An old Chevy pickup was parked in the driveway of a small boxlike structure. The exterior of the little house was stucco, grey, and crumbling. The windows were square and unimaginative, the door painted candy apple red.

Davy released his seatbelt and leaned forward. "This is where Pablo lives? Cool," he said, when a giant black Lab bounded out of the front door, followed closely by his friend and a woman who looked surprised and a little unsure when all three of them climbed from the car.

"Hello, Carlita," Margaret greeted, holding out her hand to the woman. "I'm Margaret Parker. Thanks for letting us stop by. Davy was very worried about Pablo. He wanted to see for himself that he was all right."

"Si."

Davy was immediately knocked down by the wriggling black Labrador puppy. It licked his face and tried to crawl onto his lap, to the chagrin of Pablo, who tried to pull him away. But Davy's laughter was contagious and soon Pablo was rolling on the grass with him, wrestling with the overly exuberant puppy.

Carlita glanced worriedly at the boys, but Margaret laughed and turned toward the house. "They'll be fine. Davy loves animals. Could we go in and talk for a minute while they play?" she asked, her smile bright and carefree.

The woman hesitated, then gestured toward the front door. "Si."

She motioned for them to sit on the small, flower-print sofa and went into the adjoining kitchen to make coffee. Soon she was back, and sat in a little rocker across from them. She smiled and clasped nervous hands in her lap. She was a short woman, even shorter than her brother. Her hair was streaked with threads of grey but she didn't appear any older than forty.

Margaret was beginning to think the woman spoke no English when she suddenly blurted out, "Pablo's a good boy. He's sorry to cause so much trouble."

"He didn't cause any trouble. He was just in the wrong place at the wrong time. I'm truly sorry he was caught up in this horrible situation." Margaret smiled and leaned back on the sofa, her gaze straying to a photograph on the mantel above the television in the corner. She nudged Billie and gestured with a nod of her head. Billie's eyes opened wide and she abruptly stood up and approached the mantel.

Carlita Ortiz stood up also and tried to direct her away from the photograph, but Billie had already picked it up. "This is the Sanchez family. They owned the winery before my uncle, Jack Fredrickson." If eyes were swords, Carlita would have been pierced through. "Why do you have this picture?"

Carlita pressed her lips tightly together and shook her head back and forth as though to make the question go away. "I can't speak with you anymore," she said, waving toward the door.

"We're not leaving until you tell us what you and your brother have to do with Sean Parker and the plot to kidnap Davy!"

Margaret hoped Billie didn't shove the woman back in her chair, but from the look on her face she was that close. "Carlita," she said, intervening, her voice soft and understanding, "it's all right. I know you wouldn't do anything to hurt Davy." She glanced out the front window and saw the boys still playing with the dog. "You and Mario are part of the Sanchez family, aren't you?"

Carlita continued to wring her hands, but she gave a small nod.

The admission clearly floored Billie. "What?"

"Adam and I were looking at the photographs last night and realized that Mario looks very much like this man." Margaret pointed at the elder Sanchez. "He's your father, isn't he?" she asked Carlita.

"Si. There's just me and Mario now. He told me if Juan and I did what he asked we would all be able to stay in America. He purchased papers for them. My husband and son are not legal," she blurted, unable to keep the secrets bottled up any longer. Her eyes were filled with misery. "I didn't want to help that man get out of prison, but Mario said it was for the best. He's never gotten over Martina's death."

"Martina?" The name was but a breath from Billie's lips.

"Si," the woman nodded, "Tina was our baby sister. She was only twelve when we lived at the winery. Papa found out she was pregnant. He was furious, but she wouldn't tell who the father was. She just cried all the time." Her eyes welled up and she sniffed. "Papa decided we had to move. He couldn't have everyone know that his daughter was a whore. So we went back to Mexico."

"And what happened to Tina?" Billie asked, her voice gentled with understanding.

"Tina and the baby died. She was just too small to give birth." She drew a breath and slowly released it, her face crumpling with the memories. "Mario found out that Sean Parker was the father. That he had raped her." She wiped a tear from her cheek. "He swore he would kill him someday."

Margaret was baffled. "If he hated my father so much, why would he help him get out of prison?" And then the answer exploded in her mind. Mario wanted to kill Sean—personally. He couldn't wait for time or another inmate to do the job for him. Mario Sanchez was playing the part of a vigilante.

"Mario and Sean were friends when we lived at the winery. So he felt like he was stabbed in the heart twice," Carlita said, sitting back in the rocker. She looked down at her lap.

"Where did they go?" Billie asked.

"Mexico. My brother belongs to the cartel now. He will make Sean Parker suffer many times over for what he did," she said, beginning to rock back and forth, the chair making a thumping sound against the thin carpet.

Margaret saw fear in the woman's eyes, in her hunched shoulders. Her brother had turned into the monster he sought. The sins of the fathers were far-reaching indeed. Billie touched her arm, and inclined her head toward the door.

"Thank you, Carlita," she said.

"You won't turn us in?" the woman pleaded, lifting her arms toward them. "If we go back they will take Pablo and make him into a killer. That is why we left. Mario said it was the only way to keep him safe."

Margaret met the woman's frightened gaze and shook her head.

She followed Billie outside.

Davy wasn't ready to leave yet, but he reluctantly climbed in the backseat. Pablo stood in the yard, waving them off. "Are we ever going to see Pablo again?" he asked.

"I don't know, Davy." Margaret turned in the front seat and gave him a soft smile. "Sometimes we only have a short time with people we care about, and then they're gone." Thoughts of Agosto came to mind. Sometime soon she would have to have that conversation with her son.

Billie drove out of the neighborhood, keeping her thoughts to herself. But once they were cruising along on the highway toward home, she glanced over. "Are you all right?" she asked.

Margaret knew what she meant. She didn't have an answer. Finding out that a member of the Mexican Cartel had a vendetta against her father was mind boggling. Sean Parker was an evil man who had destroyed many lives. He was also her father. She didn't want to imagine what his sins had finally wrought.

CHAPTER SIXTEEN

"Welcome!" Antonio greeted them at the door of the restaurant, his eyes straying toward Billie's mother. His smile stretched wide when he caught her eye. "Sabrina. You've come back to me."

She took male attention like a seasoned veteran. "If it wasn't such a horribly long flight, I'd come back more often—to see my daughter of course." She let him kiss her on the cheek, before sweeping past him into the dining room. Her sapphire blue knee-length dress sparkled with the glint of sequins along the neckline, accentuating dark hair and creamy skin. Margaret was amazed that she appeared so young.

The restaurant was closed to the public, allowing Carl to throw Handel and Billie an elaborate engagement celebration. In a white tuxedo Carl moved about the room greeting each guest, the perfect host. He and his brother Antonio reminded Margaret just a bit too much of their cousin Agosto in looks and manner. But unlike Agosto, their suave, handsome looks were only frosting on their true personalities. Both of them were teddy bears, lovers of women, but gentlemen through and through.

"Would you like a glass of champagne?" Adam stood at her elbow in a black suit and emerald green silk tie, a fluted glass in each hand. His auburn hair was parted on the side and combed back.

"Thank you." Her gaze strayed to the happy couple. Handel and Billie were already on the dance floor, moving together to the slow seductive strains of a Rumba.

"You look amazing," Adam said, clearly enjoying the sight of her in a dress after seeing her in nothing but jeans and t-shirts for the past week. She'd taken special pains to pick just the right one, something feminine, a bit alluring, and apparently his favorite color. Emerald green. He did look pleased.

Carl made a "lets get this party started" motion toward the D.J. he'd hired for the night, and the man pumped up the music with a Brittany Spears heart-thumping dance tune. Handel glanced up and shook his head. He grinned and pulled Billie laughing from the floor.

"Handel's too chicken to try that one," Billie said, out of breath. Her dark hair swung around her face and he gently pushed it away, then leaned in and kissed her.

"I'm not chicken. I just prefer dancing close to the woman I love."

Margaret glanced at Adam, and imagined he felt as she did. They were the third and fourth wheels on a Tandem bicycle. "Want to dance?" she asked, raising her voice to be heard over the music.

"Thought you'd never ask." He took her hand and they moved out to the dance floor.

She spotted Davy up on the stage, watching the DJ and asking questions. When she tucked him in bed tonight he'd probably tell her he'd changed his mind about the wine vintner gig and now wanted to be a DJ. She smiled when he looked up and saw them dancing together. He grinned and waved.

Carl made his famous tortellini with asparagus and garlic cream sauce and served Margaret's Wine with dinner. Everyone had to get up and give a toast, sharing thoughts or best wishes for the happy couple.

Sabrina Fredrickson finally stood, raised her glass, and smiled at everyone around the table. "If it weren't for Davy, I might not be here tonight. Sometimes it takes tragedy to bring families together, and although we don't enjoy going through those times, we end up stronger in the end. My beautiful daughter, Wilhelmina, is a true example of having been refined in the fire. Now Margaret has been tested and proven as well." She glanced toward Adam and raised her brows. "I don't think I have to tell one young man here tonight what a prize she would make."

Everybody laughed, except Adam, who turned apologetic eyes toward Margaret. She smiled and reached for his hand under the edge of the tablecloth.

Sabrina continued. "To Handel and Billie. May your love burn as bright as the California sun, be strong enough to pull you through any rough patches and fertile enough to give me many grandchildren."

She took her seat amid loud and raucous applause. Antonio, sitting on her right, leaned in brushing his fingers along her neck and whispered something in her ear. Margaret wondered if Sabrina might be the next Fredrickson to fall for a California lover.

The DJ started up the music again with Neil Diamond's classic *September Morn*. It seemed appropriate. It was late September and half past midnight already. Margaret looked at Adam and inclined her head toward the dance floor. He pulled out her chair and took her hand.

Sally and Loren were already swaying together. Sally's head only came up to his chest but he didn't seem to mind. He playfully spun her around and pulled her back in close, his chin resting atop her head. She wrapped her arms around him and held on for the ride.

"Look at them. Complete opposites, but totally meant for each other."

Adam smiled. "Sounds like what you told me about winemaking. It takes just the right amount of acidity and sugar content to make the perfect wine." His gaze was relentless. "How do you think we fare? Too sweet? Too acidic? Or just right?"

"Time will tell. A few more months to go through clarification and fermentation and if we're lucky we might just have a lovely, complex, but well-balanced relationship."

"Is that how it's going to be? Everything relating to wine?"

She shrugged. "It's my life."

"Well music is my life and I just made up a song for you."

"Just now?"

"Well, we were sitting at the table a really long time," he said, his voice teasing.

He started to sing in a soft gravelly whisper, getting a little louder as he really got into it.

"I fell in love with a West coast girl,
In the southern California world
She turned my northern mind awhirl,
Made me say some things and I acted the fool
Yeah, I'm a little bit drunk on Margaret's wine,
Margaret's wine, Margaret's wine
Cause she crushed my heart, but it turned out fine
Margaret's Wine, Margaret's wine
Yeah, I'm a little bit drunk on Margaret's wine"

He dragged the last word out and looked surprised when he got a ripple of applause from those on the dance floor near enough to overhear him. Margaret felt the color rise in her face and she pressed it against his chest, laughing.

He pulled her to a quiet corner away from the others. "So what do you think?"

She shook her head, a soft smile on her lips. "I think you're more than a little bit drunk on Margaret's wine."

He leaned close enough to kiss her but stopped a breath away. "Yet I still crave more." He pressed his lips to hers and drank deep.

***

There was a package on Billie's desk when she returned from lunch Monday afternoon. She picked it up. No return address, but it was postmarked, Juarez, Mexico. She bit her bottom lip and ripped open the seal. Inside was the bundle of Polaroids – minus one. Martina Sanchez.

ABOUT THE AUTHOR

Barbara is the author of *Entangled*, the first Fredrickson Winery novel. She grew up on a small farm in Washington State but now lives in the mean "burbs" of Minnesota with her husband and their dogs, Rugby and Willow. With her kids now pushed out of the nest and encouraged to fly, Barbara spends time writing, collecting books, and riding motorcycles with her husband in pursuit of her next story.